Also by Rohan Gavin

Knightley & Son
Knightley & Son: K-9

KNIGHTLEY&
SON
3 OF A KIND

ROHAN GAVIN

BLOOMSBURY

NEW YORK   LONDON   OXFORD   NEW DELHI   SYDNEY

First published in Great Britain in January 2016 by Bloomsbury Publishing Plc
Published in the United States of America in August 2016
by Bloomsbury Children's Books
www.bloomsbury.com

Bloomsbury is a registered trademark of Bloomsbury Publishing Plc

For information about permission to reproduce selections from this book, write to
Permissions, Bloomsbury Children's Books, 1385 Broadway, New York, New York 10018
Bloomsbury books may be purchased for business or promotional use. For information on
bulk purchases please contact Macmillan Corporate and Premium Sales Department at
specialmarkets@macmillan.com

Library of Congress Cataloging-in-Publication Data
Names: Gavin, Rohan, author.
Title: 3 of a kind / Rohan Gavin.
Other titles: Three of a kind
Description: New York : Bloomsbury Children's Books, 2016.
Series: Knightley and Son
Summary: When his father's loyal housekeeper goes missing, thirteen-year-old Darkus,
an extraordinary crime solver, his father, Alan, and stepsister, Tilly, go to Las Vegas
where they again face the Combination criminal organization.
Identifiers: LCCN 2015037726
ISBN 978-1-61963-830-3 (hardcover) • ISBN 978-1-61963-831-0 (e-book)
Subjects: | CYAC: Mystery and detective stories. | Missing persons—Fiction. |
Fathers and sons—Fiction. | Las Vegas (Nev.)—Fiction. | BISAC: JUVENILE FICTION/
Mysteries & Detective Stories. | JUVENILE FICTION/Humorous
Stories. | JUVENILE FICTION/Family/Multigenerational.
Classification: LCC PZ7.G2357 Aam 2016 | DDC [Fic]—dc23
LC record available at https://lccn.loc.gov/2015037726

Typeset by RefineCatch Limited, Bungay, Suffolk
Printed and bound in the U.S.A. by Berryville Graphics Inc., Berryville, Virginia
2 4 6 8 10 9 7 5 3 1

For my mum & dad, who inspired this series

KNIGHTLEY&
SON
3 OF A KIND

PROLOGUE
THE GAME BEGINS

Private detective Alan Knightley looked perfectly ordinary, apart from the excessive display of tweed, the thousand-yard stare, and the fact that he was talking to himself.

"I read you," he whispered into a tiny microphone that extended from under the brim of his hat by his left sideburn, relaying the message to his junior partner. Moments later, Knightley received a response through an equally tiny speaker in his ear canal. He listened carefully before replying, "Copy that. Target's on the move."

Knightley moved stealthily out of the café on Baker Street and tipped his hat in the direction of the neighboring town house, number 221b—once home to another great detective. Then he walked down the busy thoroughfare toward the even busier Marylebone Road, where the rain gave way to sunshine.

Ahead of him was another middle-aged man, of medium height and medium build, with short-clipped dark hair, dark glasses, dark suit, and a dark trench coat. The man

1

walked with a strangely eccentric confidence, drawing no attention, despite the occasional twitch of his shoulder, which Knightley knew all too well as part of the pattern of nerves and impulses that made up his archnemesis: Morton Underwood. For Underwood was the head of the shadowy crime organization the Combination; a villain who had apparently died under the wheels of a train in the London Underground, only to return from the dead when forensics connected him to known crime boss (and suspected were-wolf) the now deceased Barabas King.

Underwood turned the corner, heading east on Marylebone Road, moving at a fair pace, although Knightley was certain the man didn't know he was being followed.

Passing a row of plate-glass windows, Knightley used the reflection to scan the surrounding pedestrians, but none of them appeared to notice him. The bystanders all stared ahead, and the London traffic crawled along indifferently.

So it appeared the intelligence that Knightley had received was correct. The subject was alone, unguarded—at least for now—and carrying out a private and personal errand.

In fact, this was something of a personal errand for Knightley too—for the man in his sights was once a close family friend, a college pal who had even played godfather to Knightley's beloved son, Darkus.

But that was before Underwood's descent into darkness and criminality. It was Underwood's hypnotic powers that had put Knightley in a four-year coma, resulting in the loss of many of his detective faculties; and it was Underwood who was—inadvertently—the reason for young Darkus's unlikely rise to fame with the birth of the detective agency Knightley & Son. Although the fate of that agency was now hanging in the balance . . . After their last case, the Knightleys were in crisis, and the sinister Combination had continued to cast a vast criminal net across London, Europe, and perhaps the entire globe.

Just as predicted, after five minutes, Underwood turned right onto Harley Street, home to some of the country's most eminent doctors. Knightley carried on past the intersection (to ensure *he* wasn't being followed), then took the next right, accelerating to a jog as he looped around the elegant buildings—all packed with consulting rooms specializing in everything from terminal disease to hair regrowth. Knightley found himself approaching Harley Street from another angle. Sure enough, Underwood's polished brogues marched into view at a set of traffic lights, and Knightley ducked behind a doorway to avoid detection. The villain crossed the road, his shoulder flinching as an SUV passed him a little too fast for his liking. Knightley emerged from his vantage point and tailed him at a discreet distance.

Underwood arrived at a tall, stone-fronted edifice with a column of brass intercoms by the heavy front door. He checked the time on a pocket watch attached to his vest,

3

then extended a gloved finger and pressed the top button. After a few seconds the door buzzed open, and Underwood stepped inside and out of sight.

"The fox is in the hole," Knightley said into his mic. "Over to you."

Underwood entered the doctor's waiting room without removing his dark glasses. He chose a corner chair and examined the other patients through his tinted lenses: a Middle Eastern couple; a white man in his thirties wearing red trousers; and in a far corner a younger girl with blond pigtails and painful-looking braces, her head in earphones, her face buried in a smartphone. Underwood made no expression and stared ahead at a gilt-edged mirror hanging on the opposite wall.

A minute later, a young receptionist entered the room and asked quietly: "Mr. Jones?"

Underwood forced a smile, adjusted his dark glasses, and followed her out of the room. The other patients didn't look up from their business. Except for the young blond girl, who pocketed her smartphone, shrugged on a backpack, and walked out into the corridor.

"Excusth me?" she lisped through her braces at the receptionist. "Isth there a bathroom around?"

"Next floor up," the receptionist answered.

At the other end of the corridor, Underwood entered the elevator and prodded a button. The door closed, and the cables whirred to life.

"Thankths," the girl replied and started up the stairs.

Reaching a landing, the girl took out her smartphone and began feverishly tapping a series of commands with one hand while removing the braces and the pigtails with the other, then slipping them into a pocket.

"Knightley, are you in position?" she whispered into the mic on her earphones.

"Ten-four, Tilly. I've gained access through the basement. I'm on my way."

"Well, don't hang about. I'm overriding the elevator car now." Tilly Palmer tapped her smartphone screen again and an activity ball spun, sending the signal. She might be Darkus Knightley's errant stepsister, and somewhat lacking in grace, but she made up for it in guile and savvy.

Inside the ascending elevator, Underwood watched the numbers illuminate one by one until the floor jolted a bit, causing him to look down. A moment later, the doors opened onto what he believed was the fourth floor. He walked past the usual potted tropical plant to the door with the familiar brass plate bearing the words: *Dr. Verbosa— Royal College of Speech Therapy.*

Underwood knocked once and turned the handle to let himself in.

"Take a seat!" the doctor answered from a high-backed leather chair, which had been rotated to face the London skyline—concealing his identity.

Underwood squinted under his glasses. The doctor appeared to be tending to a window box, but Underwood could have sworn there wasn't usually a window box there. The wide mirror on the wall to his right was new too.

"I—I apologize for m-missing our last appointment," Underwood explained with his trademark stutter. "Some trouble at work. I've been p-practicing the exercises you taught me."

"Nae bother," replied the doctor, in what appeared to be a Scottish accent.

"Doctor Verbosa . . . ?" Underwood inquired, his suspicions raised, his hand reaching for an inside pocket.

The high-backed chair swiveled around, creaking under the weight, to reveal the corduroy-clad bulk of Uncle Bill, also known as Montague Billoch, from Scotland Yard's secretive SO42: Specialist Operations branch 42—also known in the highest circles as the Department of the Unexplained. Not an uncle by blood but a cherished member of the Knightleys' crime-solving family, Bill held a .38 revolver trained directly on Underwood's chest.

"A'right, hands where ah can see 'em," the Scottish detective announced in his thick Highland brogue. "Doctor Verbosa's still waiting for ye one floor down, ye big balloon. We mucked about wi' the elevator."

Underwood spun and lunged for the door, until it opened by itself and he ran into a wall of Donegal tweed in the shape of Alan Knightley.

"Hello, old pal," Knightley managed, breathless, as he manhandled Underwood back into the privacy of the consulting room and locked the door behind them.

"A-Alan, what a pleasant surprise," Underwood fawned, then looked back at the mirror spanning one side of the room. "I see what's going on now."

"Observation was never your shortcoming," said Knightley, frisking Underwood from head to toe for weapons. "Morality, on the other hand . . ." Knightley removed a silenced handgun and a switchblade and slung them onto the desk in front of Uncle Bill, who inspected them clinically, as if he were still playing the part of doctor. Knightley forcefully sat Underwood down in the patient's chair. "We thought you died under that Tube train. I almost felt sorry for you. I suppose it was all a simple misdirection. A trick of the light."

"Something like that." Underwood removed his clip-on shades to reveal a pair of Coke-bottle glasses that made his eyes distort and float like saucers.

Knightley tried to ignore the villain's gaze, knowing it could be hazardous to his health. "You and your forces of darkness have caused me and my family a lot of trouble and strife," he went on. "Not to mention showing an extremely *casual* approach to our personal safety."

"In other words, you're a murderin' bahookie," Bill added,

dropping the weapons into evidence bags and concealing them in his massive overcoat before putting on his homburg hat to indicate he meant business.

"Your incarceration will be as long and painful as the law permits," Knightley warned. "But not before we've extracted the information we require to bring the Combination to justice."

"Hmm," replied Underwood and lightly adjusted his seat to face the mirror. "Is that Darkus in there, I wonder?" he muttered, as if to himself. "No . . . he would f-face me in person. So the junior detective must be . . . otherwise engaged. In that case, it must be Tilly, his faithful—if damaged—stepsister. Like a hound on the scent. Desperate for answers about who killed her mother, Carol . . . Alan's f-former assistant. Fathers and sons, mothers and daughters. Blood really does run deep."

Behind the mirror, Tilly stood in a makeshift viewing room, watching through the two-way mirror, her fists clenched by her sides. A female police officer stood next to her for protection as the voices echoed through an intercom speaker.

"I'd advise you to be quiet about that," Knightley threatened, his eyes glittering.

"Would you care to settle this with a game, Alan?" the villain piped up. "A game of wits? A game of chance?"

"What is there to settle? You lost. We won," declared Knightley.

"It'll be like the old days," said Underwood. "Only this

time I'm not talking about chess. And I f-fear you may need your son's assistance again, if you have any hope of a successful outcome."

"You're in no position to play games," Knightley responded.

Underwood shrugged, turning back to the mirror, seeing only his own reflection. "What if I told you that I had information ab-bout your mother's death, Tilly? Information that has up until now b-been withheld from you? Then would *you* play my little game?"

Behind the two-way mirror, Tilly's eyes narrowed as she minutely shook her head, not daring to believe him.

Underwood calmly reached for his vest. Uncle Bill cocked his pistol by way of warning.

"He's clean," Knightley assured the Scotsman.

Underwood merely took out his pocket watch and observed the time, then swung it gently on its chain while gazing at the mirror through his thick lenses. "Very well. The offer stands. Play the game and find the truth."

Tilly watched the proceedings from behind the glass, her eyes narrowing further. "Wait a second . . ."

Underwood gazed at his own reflection, his enlarged eyes following the pocket watch traveling back and forth, back and forth, back and forth.

"No—!" Tilly shouted.

Suddenly, the mirror in the doctor's office exploded as a chair hurtled through it from the other side. The police officer tried to restrain Tilly, but the teen had already kicked out the remains of the safety glass and stepped through, spraying the room and its occupants with gem-like fragments. Underwood sat perfectly still, with the pocket watch still swinging from his hand like a pendulum.

"He's hypnotizing *himself*!" cried Tilly, scrambling toward him.

Knightley and Bill surged forward, but it was too late. The pocket watch dropped to the carpet, the chain snaking around it.

Underwood's arms fell limp and his eyes glazed over, freezing a smile on his grim, skull-like face.

Tilly grabbed the man by his necktie and throttled him. "Don't you go to sleep on me . . . Don't you *dare*—"

Underwood's eyes stared ahead blankly, but his mouth continued to function for a moment, mumbling something: "F-fifty-three, sixty-four, chance, a relay, thirteen-thirty-n-nine."

Tilly raised her smartphone, tapping the numbers onto the screen. "It's a code," she stammered excitedly. "Damn it, it's a code."

Underwood's mouth fell ajar, and he lost consciousness altogether.

"Aye, but meaning what?" asked Bill.

"I don't know," confessed Knightley.

"We need Darkus . . . ," Tilly stated plainly.

"Aye," agreed Bill and set about cuffing Underwood's limp hands together behind the back of the chair.

"You know Doc and I are not currently on speaking terms," Knightley complained.

"Then you'd better get back on speaking terms, and fast," barked Tilly. "He didn't come home last night, which is *very* unlike him. Semester's over, so he can't be at school. You're his father. *Find him!*"

CHAPTER 1
NETHERWORLDS

Darkus burst through the bushes, losing his footing and tearing the elbow of his herringbone overcoat. Blood coursed from a laceration on his arm as he emerged from the undergrowth into the soft, wet grass of a lush meadow that was veiled in ominous shadow. He saw a pair of trees intertwined in a devil's fork and ran toward them. Then the howl arrived again, even louder and more chilling than before. It was followed by a rapid snapping of twigs as the creature raced through the woods behind him, its paws barely touching the ground.

Under the devil's fork was a large pond, shimmering in the moonlight. He turned back, seeing the low, dark shape of the creature hovering across the meadow in his direction—a matter of seconds away from catching him. Darkus stumbled toward the pond and began wading into the murky water, which quickly crept up over his brogues, his overcoat, his tweed three-piece suit, and up to his neck. Darkus tried to swim, but the weight of his clothes was holding him back. He struggled through the water, getting some way from the shore. Then he turned back to look at the creature, but it had been replaced by an altogether different animal. But it wasn't possible. This animal was deceased.

It was his beloved German shepherd, Wilbur, wagging his tail, watching from dry land, holding his leash in his mouth as he always did, shaking his snout to beckon him back.

"No . . . ," said Darkus, feeling the current dragging him under. "No, Wilbur's gone. He's *dead*."

Tears started rolling down his face. Until they were met by the black pond water bubbling up around his neck, seeping into the corners of his mouth and finally consuming him completely.

Darkus's head lurched forward, then he sat up, embarrassed, wiping the tears from his face. He was wearing a gray sweatshirt, blue jeans, and sneakers. He was surrounded by half a dozen teenagers, most wearing goth clothing, some with mascara, guyliner, and nose piercings. They all sat in a circle in a darkened room, lit by a single candle flickering in the center.

"That was very good, Doc," a girl's voice whispered from beside him.

"It's not Doc . . . it's *Darkus*," he answered firmly.

"Okay, Darkus," said the girl and turned her face to the candlelight to reveal Alexis Bateman, his fellow classmate and former editor of *The Cranston Star*. Since their near-fatal encounter with the monstrous Barabas King on Hampstead Heath, Alexis's blond hair had turned permanently gray. But she tied it up neatly, and Darkus thought it suited her. Gone were her customary raincoat, reporter bag, and black cigarette pants, having been replaced more recently by a tailored tweed ensemble that was distinctly Knightley-esque, complete with a walking hat worn at a jaunty angle. "Do you want to tell us more?" she inquired gently. "You're among friends here."

"No. Not right now," Darkus answered self-consciously. "I don't work for the school newspaper anymore, remember?"

"And I don't conduct private investigations anymore," he replied. "Especially when the subject of that investigation is me."

"Guided meditation isn't supposed to be easy. You're getting in touch with deeper forces beyond our understanding. Extrasensory perception, the spirit world—call it what you will. You can even talk to the dead . . . or so they say."

Darkus knew all about the outlandish promises of the supernatural, having heard them from his equally outlandish father. He also knew their dangers. Having weighed the possibilities, Darkus remained a disciple of *reason*. But the fact that he'd even agreed to this exercise was evidence that all reasonable self-help methods had been exhausted.

"Guided meditation, lucid dreaming, whatever it is," said Darkus. "I thought it would give me answers, but it's only raised more questions . . . like who I am and what I'm supposed to be doing with my life. I'm sorry, Lex, but this whole thing, it's not for me. If you'll excuse me . . ."

Darkus got to his feet, picked up his distinctly un-Knightley-esque parka, and left the circle, crossing the bare wooden floor of the deserted, boarded-up Gothic house and descending the creaky staircase, stepping over the gaps where bits were missing.

Darkus used his shoulder to shove open the front door, exiting into a derelict lot painted orange by the fading evening light.

"Darkus, wait—" Alexis caught up with him. "I was just trying to help. I owe you my life, remember?"

She curled a gray lock of hair under her hat and flashed him the cockeyed smile that had managed to stay intact through her trauma and the months of therapy that followed it. She had, without a doubt, fared better than their other classmate, Brendan Doyle, whose mauling at the hands of King's attack dogs had left the boy still recovering at an undisclosed clinic somewhere.

"I don't think we should hang out anymore, Lex. I'm sorry." He looked for the right words. "It's just too much of a reminder of the past."

She fell silent for a beat. "Okay," she answered, crestfallen. "If that's what you want."

Darkus nodded sadly and walked across a garden that had been left to ruin. He vanished under a row of sycamore trees and into the shadows.

Alexis removed her hat and watched him go.

The house party was in full swing. Electronic dance music reverberated through the modern, glass-fronted home as Darkus crossed the lawn, approaching the front door. He pressed the intercom and heard a bottle smash—which was presumably unrelated. A few moments later the door opened to reveal the host: Darkus's teenage classmate Jason, an acquaintance more than a friend, decked out in an over-sized baseball cap and baggy, drop-crotch pants.

Jason did a double take. "Oh . . . my . . . God. Are we talking a flat tire, an alien abduction, or did hell just freeze over? It's the legendary Darkus Knightley, PI, in the house. Check it out." A cluster of other youths crowded around the doorway.

"Thought I'd take you up on your invitation," said Darkus. "To celebrate the summer break," he clarified.

"Of course, by all means," replied the host and ushered him into the entrance hall, which was heaving with bodies. "As long as you're off duty," he said with a wink.

"That's why I'm here," replied Darkus.

"Well, this is what we here on earth call a 'party.' Can I get you a drink?"

"Do you have lime cordial?"

"We have anything you require. Guys, you heard the man. On the rocks. And take him to the VIP area."

Beyond the hallway, two reception rooms were packed with revelers. Darkus's powers of observation (which could not so easily be switched off) instantly detected an average age of fifteen, a range of ethnicities, and a preponderance of skin rather than clothing.

As he was led through the party, he felt his catastrophizer ticking and humming in time to the music. The catastrophizer was Darkus's friend and his enemy. It allowed him to continually digest potential clues taken from his immediate surroundings, and it always suggested the worst-case scenario. Of course, most of the time, the worst-case scenario was *not* the case, and there was a much more mundane and ordinary explanation. But occasionally, for example on the first two Knightley & Son investigations, the catastrophizer served up the cold, unvarnished truth.

However, that was past history now. He and his dad were not currently speaking, due to the catastrophic end to the Barabas King case (the Case of the Hampstead Heath Howler, as his father had named it; or K-9, as Darkus called it). Rightly or wrongly, Darkus held his father responsible for what had happened on that fateful full moon. Prior to forming Knightley & Son, his father had been absent for those four long years, confined to a coma by the hypnotic powers of Morton Underwood. But his dad had been absent long *before* that as well, when he'd confined himself to his office, working day and night and slowly losing his wife and family in the process. Darkus had essentially grown up without a father, until his dad had returned—virtually back from the dead—as a partner in crime-solving, bringing much-needed adventure into Darkus's life, but not the level of intimacy or affection that a son might wish for from a parent. Plus, his dad never warned him about the profound loss that comes with devoting one's life to detective work. And Darkus never really had any other choice in life, with the catastrophizer continually gnawing at his mind. He was always going to follow in his father's footsteps, and his father had never been around to tell him not to.

Darkus returned his mind to the present as he was led up a glass staircase, underlit by discreet LED lights. Darkus knew Jason's parents were wealthy and traveled a lot, leaving their son to throw regular parties that incensed the neighbors; but the gatherings were expertly cleaned up afterward, with the precision of a criminal cleaning up a crime scene, erasing any trace of the party's existence. It was even rumored that the host made cash payments to the neighbors in return for their silence.

Darkus was led across a minstrel gallery that overlooked the main reception room, where over a hundred kids were dancing with their hands raised in the air, waving plastic cups. On the far side, one brave parent had come along and was doing some embarrassing "Dad dancing" in front of the fireplace with great enthusiasm, his beard and glasses at odds with the fashionable Day-Glo and spandex on display.

The group of baseball caps escorted Darkus from the gallery to an outdoor balcony overlooking a swimming pool that was glowing blue in the night. One of Jason's minions poured Darkus a soft drink from an improvised bar consisting of a white linen cloth and an assortment of bottles. Several of the cooler kids in his grade were lined up, sucking an indeterminate green liquid through straws. A group of girls flocked together at the opposite end of the deck, glancing at Darkus and whispering to one another. It was hard to tell whether the comments were negative or positive. Having never mastered lip-reading, Darkus was unable to understand what was being said, and their body language was equally baffling.

Far easier to read were the two boys who were scaling the tiled parapet roof beside the VIP area overlooking the pool, which lay a distance of some twelve yards from the house.

"Go on, do it," one dared the other, pointing toward the alluring body of blue water.

"In your dreams. *You* do it."

The water was shimmering and inviting.

"Okay," the first one replied.

Darkus put down his cup, left the throng, and approached the parapet. His eyes narrowed as he estimated the distance from the roof to the pool, the uncertain purchase of the boys' shoes on the slate tiles, Newton's laws of motion, and the relative velocity that would have to be achieved to land safely in the water. The outlook was not encouraging.

"Erm, guys?" Darkus ventured. "I think you'll find the laws of gravity make the odds of a successful landing approximately thirty to one . . . at best."

"*Shut up, Dorkus!*"

"In that case, would you consider waiting long enough for us to create an improvised safety cushion to prevent serious injury or loss of life?"

Jason glanced up from the garden below and waved his hands around. "Get off of there. Dad'll have a fit if those tiles come loose."

Climber One looked at the other and grinned. "Okay, who's going first?"

Realizing their judgment was seriously impaired, Darkus addressed the host. "I suggest calling the emergency services. Specify *two* ambulances."

"Seriously?!" Jason yelled up again. "Get off of there, or I'm never inviting you again. Ever!"

Climber Two nodded to his friend. "Maybe it's not such a great idea."

"Yeah, maybe you're right," Climber One replied, then involuntarily yelped "Agh—!!" He suddenly lost his footing and slid clattering down the ledge by the VIP area in a tangle of arms and legs. It would have looked like a comedy routine if there hadn't been a free fall of fifteen yards below him.

Revelers on the balcony and around the pool started screaming. The host stood frozen in horror.

Climber Two started down after his friend, but set off a minor avalanche of slate tiles that rattled down the incline and flew over the edge in quick succession, shattering loudly on the ground. Climber Two grabbed onto a chimney for dear life, while Climber One tripped over the loose slates, appearing to tap-dance, before cartwheeling down the remainder of the roof and dropping into the abyss.

Until a hand shot out and grabbed his arm.

"*Dorkus!* What are you doing?" The climber stared up in shock.

"Saving you. And it's *Darkus* . . ."

The climber slipped again and screamed until Darkus gripped the boy's wrist and wedged himself against the corner of the metal balcony—using his father's preferred martial art, Wing Chun, to plant his feet instead of following the ill-fated mountaineer over the edge. But the force of gravity was too strong. The climber clawed onto Darkus's arm. The sole of Darkus's Dunlop Green Flash sneaker slipped on the wooden deck, and he lost his balance, toppling over the railing.

"No—!" the climber shouted as he saw his earnest classmate following him into space . . .

Until another pair of hands shot out and grabbed Darkus around the waist. Darkus maintained his grip on the climber and craned his neck, seeing the embarrassing dad from the dance floor, hyperventilating and heaving both boys back over the railing. Darkus held on tight as the three of them tumbled back onto the safety of the balcony.

The revelers gasped, catching their breath.

"I assume your mother knows you're here," the rescuer announced.

Darkus knew that voice. He did a double take and looked up to see his father standing over him, partially obscured by the fake beard and glasses.

"Dad—?" Darkus exclaimed, eyes wide. "I can't believe . . ."—his voice turned to an accusatory whisper— "you'd *embarrass* me like this."

"Would you rather I let you fall?" Knightley protested. "The chances of survival were approximately thirty to one. At best."

Darkus shook his head and got to his feet. "Not here, Dad. Please." He walked from the balcony into the house.

Knightley followed his son around the minstrel gallery with the partygoers gyrating below as if nothing had happened. "I know you don't want to see me . . . but I need to see *you*, Doc. It's important."

He spun. "It's *Darkus*."

Knightley recoiled, then straightened up, looking hurt. "As you wish." He trailed Darkus down the glass staircase, through the entrance hall, and out the front door.

Knightley caught up with him on the grass, until Darkus turned to block him.

"How did you find me?"

"Tilly did a sweep of social media. 'Jason's summer pool party,' I believe," said Knightley, using finger quotes, then winced as he peeled the fake beard from his face. "You've been spending an inordinate amount of time online lately," he said disapprovingly.

"You mean, like every other kid my age?"

"I would question the assumption that you're anything like other children in any way, Darkus." Knightley glanced at the revelers stumbling aimlessly around them.

"Well, at least I'm trying . . ."

Knightley looked truly puzzled by this, as if the prospect of "normal" was something to be avoided at all costs. "I suppose that would explain the outfit," he deduced, casting a disparaging eye over Darkus's casual clothes and shoes before returning to business. "The reason I'm here is I have a message for you . . . from Tilly."

"Since when have you become her errand boy?"

"Well . . . ," Knightley mumbled. "Well, we've sort of been working together, as a matter of fact," he confessed, and shrugged apologetically.

Darkus's jaw dropped. "You mean, like"—this time he was the one using finger quotes—"'Knightley and . . . surrogate daughter'?"

His father shrugged again. "Something like an apprentice, you might say."

Darkus's face ran the gamut of emotions from disbelief through amazement to bewilderment—coming to rest on betrayal.

"She's unpredictable," warned Darkus. "A wild card. You said it yourself."

"Since you took your sabbatical, she's the only card I've got." Knightley paused, looking for any hint of forgiveness. "Before you shoot the messenger, don't you want to hear what the message is?"

Darkus turned away and walked toward the road.

"We've apprehended Morton Underwood," his father called after him.

Darkus stopped in his tracks, glancing around to make sure no one else had heard—but the party continued its noisy progress.

"The trouble is he's put himself into a posthypnotic trance," Knightley went on.

Darkus turned to face his dad, realizing the gravity of the situation.

"We have no idea how long this 'episode' might last," Knightley added. "It's a coma-like state, much the same as what he did to me. It could be years."

"Did he say anything before he entered this state?" demanded Darkus.

"He invited us to play a game. He said he had information about Tilly's mother's death. About *Carol*." Knightley's eyes winced with painful recollection for a moment before returning to their steely gaze.

"What kind of information?" said Darkus, his brow furrowing with concern.

"He recited a code of some kind." Knightley unfolded a piece of paper containing a set of words and numbers, then read from it: "Fifty-three, sixty-four, chance, a relay, thirteen-thirty-nine."

"That's exactly what he said?" asked Darkus. "I mean *precisely?*"

His father nodded.

Darkus closed his eyes and let the words and numbers whirl around his mind like balls on a roulette wheel, waiting to see where they would land. Knightley knew from experience not to disturb his son during this process. Instead he watched with a mixture of awe and the faintest hint of professional jealousy.

"Be so kind as to repeat the sequence again," said Darkus with his eyes still closed.

Knightley read the code the way a bingo caller announces the lucky numbers. "Fifty-three, sixty-four, chance . . . a relay . . . thirteen-thirty-nine."

Darkus remained silent, examining the vortex of

possibilities in his head. Then he began to speak quietly: "Once you stop trying to make sense of it and just listen to the *sounds* themselves, a familiar pattern presents itself."

Knightley raised his eyebrows. "It does?" he said, surprised.

"Yes," answered his son. "Underwood has a speech impediment that appears to have garbled what would otherwise be a perfectly comprehensible message—either spoken deliberately or by accident, before he lost consciousness."

"You mean like a slip-up of the mind. A 'brain fart,' I believe it's known as," Knightley speculated, before censuring himself: "Sorry, do proceed. How did you arrive at this deduction?"

"Simple," said Darkus. "Why else would Underwood give us the location of a safe-deposit box in central London?"

"A safe-deposit box? How could you possibly know that?"

"It's not 'chance, a relay.' It's 'Chancery Lane.' The Chancery Lane Safe-Deposit Company is the oldest and most trusted in London. The address is Fifty-Three to Sixty-Four Chancery Lane. Therefore, we can assume that the number of the safe-deposit box is identified by the remaining digits in the sequence: one-three-three-nine."

"Outstanding," said Knightley, shaking his head in admiration. "You've still got it, Doc." He guided his son toward their trusty, souped-up London black cab that was parked in the shadows.

"But you're still not getting it, Dad." Darkus resisted his father's guidance. "Consider this solution a farewell gift."

"A farewell? From what?"

"From the business. I'm not coming back to work, Dad. I've got exams next year. And a lot of catching up to do . . . in all kinds of ways."

"I'm afraid it's my turn to be rational. Tilly told me about you and Alexis, and her slightly . . . left-of-center ideas."

Darkus waited to see where this was going.

"I know this is about Wilbur," said his father gently. "I know how much it hurt you, but I never could have predicted that outcome—"

"I don't want to talk about that right now."

"I loved that mutt as much as you did."

"Did you?" Darkus challenged him, feeling his chest tighten with emotion.

"I never wanted this line of work for you, Doc. But we both have to accept that detective work's in your blood. There's no escaping it."

Darkus took a deep breath, then answered, "Congratulations on apprehending Underwood. I'm certain you'll crack the Combination soon enough. Good night, Dad."

Darkus started walking away, feeling a childish sense of victory, tempered with an unsettling, nauseous feeling in his stomach.

"The Combination is a revolving door, you know that," his father implored. "One leader falls, another takes their place. Until we get them all in one place, crack the mechanism, and take it apart, they'll always be out there. They'll never stop . . ."

"I hope you and Tilly find what you're looking for," Darkus responded before turning away.

Knightley's arms dropped to his sides and he stood on the sidewalk, hopeless, as his son passed by the familiar shape of the London black cab and walked off into the night.

CHAPTER 2
THE PUZZLE BOX

Tilly marched briskly past the row of office buildings, whose windows reflected the first rays of sunrise—which were not dissimilar to the orange tips of her hair, the remainder of which was currently dyed electric blue. Knightley struggled to keep up with her, and Uncle Bill's orthopedic loafers waddled from under his coattails. Two plainclothes SO42 agents followed at a distance, their eyes flicking left and right to evaluate their surroundings.

Tilly reached the imposing building, which occupied an entire block of Chancery Lane and was accessed by one reinforced door with a large surveillance camera angled over it. They were met by the tight-lipped manager of the depository, who looked them over quizzically.

"Allow me," explained Uncle Bill, offering up his creased leather ID wallet.

"Specialist Operations branch 42 . . . ?" the manager read aloud. "Never heard of it . . . until I got a call at four a.m. this morning."

"Well, let's just hope ye don't have to hear from us again," said Bill and barged past him into the foyer, where the two SO42 agents took up position.

Tilly and Knightley followed in Bill's wake, passing a pair of uniformed security guards. The manager scuttled along behind them.

Moments later the whole ensemble descended in a narrow elevator, which opened out onto a secure basement guarded by a giant vault door. It was forged out of layers of laminated steel welded together with rivets the size of dinner plates. The manager rose on tiptoe and typed a long sequence of numbers into a keypad, then a series of complex locking mechanisms rotated, gears engaged, pins retracted, and bars slid apart, causing the door to gradually swing open on a set of unfathomably thick hinges.

Tilly, Bill, and Knightley stepped through the huge doorway into a long corridor lined with compact-sized, individual steel boxes. Tilly walked straight to the box marked *1339* and tapped on it with a black-painted fingernail.

The manager made a show of reaching into his jacket for the master keys.

"Of course, this is highly irregular . . . ," he protested.

"I'm getting straight As in chemistry. Open it, or I'll blow the bloody door off," she warned.

Knightley and Bill exchanged a concerned glance.

The manager flushed and inserted one key into each of

the two locks, then turned them together. A click accompanied the door nudging ajar.

Tilly reached over and tore it open to reveal . . .

A rectangular drawer with a metal lid. She lifted the lid and groped around in the dark, vacuous space until her fingers found something sitting at the back: it was approximately the same size as a hardcover book, but it was slim, smooth and cold. She pulled it out.

It was a finely carved ivory *box*, with an array of cryptic-looking geometric designs covering every side of it. On closer inspection, there appeared to be characters lurking behind the maze of etched lines: a winged figure, a serpent, and a man with a forked tail. Tilly fumbled with the box, trying to locate the lid, but it wouldn't budge. She then shook it violently and raised her hands, preparing to shatter it on the steel edge of the deposit drawer.

"Wait—!" Knightley shouted, causing everyone to start. "It's not a toy." He prized it out of Tilly's determined grasp.

"Aye," agreed Uncle Bill—although he had no idea why. "Erm, what is it then?"

"It's a *puzzle box*," answered Knightley.

"So it *is* a toy—" Tilly demanded, reaching to grab it back.

"Ah-ah," insisted Knightley. "If you break it, you risk destroying what's inside. They're known to be booby-trapped."

"So let's X-ray it," Tilly countered.

Knightley shook his head. "It's lined with lead. This is no ordinary box," he whispered in awe. He turned it over in his hands, analyzing the markings. "Puzzle boxes are based on designs from the Mayans and the earliest African tribes. But this one appears to be Parisian in origin, mid-eighteenth century, one of only a dozen, if my hunch is correct. It is made up of hundreds, if not thousands, of moving parts. You might guess it's made of ivory. In fact, it's made of bone. Some say . . . human bone."

"Okay, that is creepy," admitted Tilly.

"Aye," concurred Bill.

The manager watched in baffled silence.

Knightley went on: "Puzzle boxes were used to keep safe the darkest secrets. Conspiracy, blackmail, murder. It was even rumored that they offered a portal into other dimensions. Other realities . . ."

"You mean like wormholes?" asked Tilly, unconvinced. "Okay, now you're getting a little carried away."

"Am I?" Knightley challenged her, his ears lifting and brow lowering. "There are phenomena in this world that defy science, that defy logic. I've known this for some time, even though the rest of you think I've lost my marbles." He paused, gathering his thoughts. "Well, I may not know everything, but I do know something about this box." He held it firmly in both hands. "Now, do you want to know what's inside or not?"

"Open it," Tilly ordered.

Knightley squinted, studying the characters etched into the sides of the box. "I've seen this done once before . . . by a Benedictine monk during the Case of the Missing Habit . . ." He held it up to his right ear and tilted it, listening to the inner workings. Then he gripped it with all ten fingers arranging themselves in a wide spread around the box, placing his fingertips on the faces of several of the figures. He then pressed firmly and twisted his hands, as if opening a cookie jar.

Nothing happened.

"Want me to have a go?" offered Bill.

"Let me have another try," said Knightley, noticing a small, flower-like design on the center of the lid. He pressed his ear to the box again, then kept the fingers of his left hand arranged on the characters while using the fingers of his right hand to rotate the petals of the flower—until he was rewarded with a gentle click and a steadily gaining whirr.

Knightley quickly knelt down and set the box on the floor as the device unfolded itself. The lid flipped back, and the four sides lowered with the aid of tiny springs, cogs, and wheels, opening up to reveal: another rectangular box inside—this one made of modern aluminum.

It was immediately recognizable as a hard drive.

Tilly grabbed for it and checked the ports. Then she

shrugged off her backpack, unzipped a compartment, and took out her laptop, unfolding and resting it on the shoulder pad of the manager's suit jacket.

"Excuse me . . . ?" he complained, craning his neck.

"You're excused," Tilly replied, continuing to use him as an improvised desk.

She connected her computer to the hard drive with a mini USB cable. She clicked twice, and a stream of green hieroglyphics filled the screen: a language that might as well have been Martian to Knightley and Bill.

Tilly gazed deeply into the programming code, then pressed a series of keys in conjunction with each other.

After several seconds a file appeared on-screen, with the words: *Carol Palmer—case history*.

"It's Mom . . ." Tilly swallowed.

She clicked again. An embedded image showed a woman's body laid out on a slab. Deceased.

Tilly wanted so badly to look away, but she couldn't.

She waited, frozen on the spot. "What—what is this?" she whispered. A tear cascaded down her cheek.

"I don't know," said Knightley. "Perhaps this is Underwood's version of 'the Knowledge,'" he speculated— referring to his own journals, which had been destroyed at the hands of the Combination, remaining only in the head of his beloved son, Darkus. His son, who was currently not talking to him. "Perhaps this is where Underwood buries the bodies . . . his secrets and misdeeds."

Knightley carefully laid a hand on Tilly's shoulder, until she shook it off.

"I want the names and locations of everyone involved in her death," she demanded. "I want answers."

"It might contain that and more," replied Knightley.

Suddenly the screen went blue, highlighting the color of Tilly's hair.

"What's happening?" she murmured.

A skull and crossbones flashed up in black and white over another sea of green hieroglyphics.

"Looks like he had an ace up his sleeve," observed Bill.

"He wants to play? Let's play." Tilly's eyebrows lowered, meeting in the middle to form an angry line above her nose. "This is malicious code. I need to conference in the group."

"What group?" asked Knightley.

"My hacker group," she replied. "I need more processing power and a secure Internet connection. Like, yesterday!"

The black London cab skidded to a halt on Cherwell Place, and Knightley approached the blue door marked *27*, letting Tilly and Uncle Bill in behind him.

Tilly scaled the stairs clutching the hard drive, crossed the landing, and burst into Knightley's office.

The Knightleys' faithful Polish housekeeper, Bogna, looked up from her employer's desk, somewhat guiltily. She was poised over the computer, waving the mouse in the air as if hunting for a signal. Her feather duster was propped beside her like an improvised antenna.

"Apology, Alan," she confessed. "You said I could use computer when you're out on assignment."

"No need to apologize, Bogna," Knightley responded quickly. "Tilly needs to hop on there now."

Bogna put down the mouse, quickly dusted some trinkets that needed urgent attention, then made way for Tilly. Uncle Bill wheezed as he reached the top of the stairs, then waved awkwardly.

"A'right, Boggers? Long time nae see."

"Yes, Monty. It has been long times." She adjusted her generously sized housecoat.

Knightley glanced from Bill to Bogna, then back again, sensing a certain electricity in the air.

Tilly slumped into Knightley's chair and hunched over the computer tower, plugging in the hard drive. "Fortunately I made some enhancements to your system last time I was here."

"You did?" asked Knightley, watching, clueless, as Tilly played the computer keys with the grace of a concert pianist. "Thanks for letting me know."

Tilly cleared several search windows that Bogna had opened.

Knightley watched with curiosity. "If you don't mind me asking, Bogna . . . what exactly were you doing on there?"

"Finding husbands," she replied flatly.

Knightley cocked his head, thinking he must have misheard. "Come again?"

"Online datings," said Bogna proudly, inspecting the fingers of her rubber gloves. "I'm not gettings any younger. And no one else is making any proposals."

Bill caught something in his throat and started coughing and blushing in equal measure. "Aye, that'll be the kipper I had this mornin'," he pointed out, before thumping the center of his chest and exhaling sharply.

"I make some sandwich," Bogna announced. "Then, if you're not needings me, Alan, I have appointments to keep." She rested the duster on her shoulder and exited the office.

Uncle Bill watched her leave, then pouted and shifted on his feet.

Knightley examined the unlikely pair, deducing that there was more going on than met the eye, but now was not the time for further investigation.

Tilly looked up from her seat. "I did a file dump." Knightley and Bill glanced at each other, confused. "I uploaded the contents of the hard drive to the dark cloud," she explained, absently playing with a letter opener.

"I know what the 'cloud' is. But what on earth is the 'dark cloud' . . . ?" Knightley asked.

"Quantum-encrypted online storage. From there, me and some colleagues can launch a multipronged attack on the code. But it'll take days. Possibly even longer." She unconsciously stabbed the letter opener into the desk in frustration.

Knightley's eyes widened until he saw she'd only punctured a stress-relief ball that he'd received several Christmases ago. He inched away from her as a precaution.

"So now," Tilly carried on, oblivious, "we wait."

Downstairs, Bogna angled a chef's knife, held the soft white bread firmly by the crust, and cut the sandwiches into triangles, not squares. Then she laid down the blade and gazed out the kitchen window at the neighboring rooftops, drifting off a moment, until her cell phone blasted its Polish folk-dance ringtone, giving her a start.

She picked up. "Bogna Rejesz? This is she?" The voice on the other end of the phone brought the hint of a smile to her face. "Ah, yes, Theo. I have received your online messages." The voice on the other end continued, causing Bogna to blush deeply and adjust the belt of her housecoat. "I would be very interested in a meetings up tonight." She listened for another few seconds. "Yes, that sounds charmings. Yes . . . you too." She ended the call and let out a long, contented sigh, before popping a clove of garlic into her mouth and chewing it dreamily.

CHAPTER 3
THE WINNER'S CIRCLE

Darkus stepped out of the chauffeur-driven limo with his mom, Jackie, close behind him. Cheers rippled through the crowd gathered outside the auditorium as bodies pressed against the security barrier by the red carpet.

"Isn't this something?" Jackie commented, awestruck. "Clive always said he'd land on his feet. I suppose I should've had more faith in him!"

"I guess," said Darkus indifferently.

He couldn't muster much enthusiasm for his stepfather Clive's sudden good fortune—and, in fact, found the man's return to fame a truly incredible turn of events. Especially since it wasn't that long ago that Clive had fallen under the spell of the Combination's hypnotic guidebook, *The Code*, and launched a murderous attack on him in the upstairs bathroom. Fortunately, that sinister book was now off the shelves, and Clive had returned to his awful—but normal—self.

"If only Tilly could see this," Jackie went on. "Have you heard from her today, Doc?"

"No," he answered, glancing guiltily at his phone, which displayed a dozen missed calls, all labeled *Tilly*.

Just then, the spectators whistled, and Darkus and his mom were politely shoved aside by a team of handlers in black T-shirts and earpieces as Clive stepped out of the limo behind them. A burst of phone cameras flashed along either side of the red carpet as the man of the hour sauntered into the spotlight.

"Fan-ruddy-tastic," murmured Clive, his salt-and-pepper hair aglow in the flashbulbs.

A female reporter sprinted over to greet him as he straightened the lapels of his extraordinarily shiny suit. A camera operator raced alongside to record the interview.

"Look at this reception," the reporter began. "Clive . . . It's week three. The talent has been chosen. Your fellow celebrity judges are already inside. How does it feel to be a fixture on Britain's highest-rated TV program?"

"It feels . . . phe-*nom*-enal"—he paused, seeking out the reporter's ID necklace resting on her blouse, before judiciously refocusing his attention on the camera—"Suzy," he added. "What can I say? It feels like . . . *destiny*."

"And I see you've brought some family members along too?" she observed.

"Them?" replied Clive. "Well, Darkus isn't really family, and my *real* daughter, Tilly . . . to be honest, the less said about her, the better."

"I see . . ." The reporter raised her eyebrows.

"Mr. Palmer?" a voice interrupted as the handlers with earpieces swarmed around him. "Let's stick to the script, huh?" one of them advised.

Clive twitched, then addressed the camera. *"The Winner's Circle* airs every Friday at eight p.m., with a results show on Saturday. Be there or be"—he drew an invisible shape in the air, then winked—*"square."*

The handlers expertly guided him across the red carpet to a discreet doorway. Clive waved vigorously to the assembled fans as he vanished into the auditorium. Darkus watched with a mixture of wonder and disbelief.

The reporter continued, "That was Clive Palmer, the disgraced former host of *Wheel Spin*, who bounced back from a nervous breakdown to land firmly in the driver's seat on the judges' panel of Britain's highest-rated TV talent contest. And I can see he hasn't changed a bit. Now, let's catch up with some of tonight's contestants . . ."

Another team of handlers escorted Jackie and Darkus to a separate entrance.

Inside, the auditorium was strangely silent. Crew members shuffled equipment around, air-conditioning units whirred from all sides, but the seats and aisles were empty, awaiting the influx of excited audience members.

Jackie and Darkus were shown to their seats in the wings, adjacent to the judges' panel.

An array of colorful spotlights and towering Jumbotron screens flickered to life. Clive strode onto the stage and took a moment to behold the spectacle, then patted down the pockets of his shiny suit, searching for something.

"This calls for a selfie," he muttered. "Debbie? What've you done with my phone?"

An anxious twentysomething assistant appeared at the edge of the stage. "I don't think you gave it to me, Mr. Palmer?"

"Are you calling me a liar, young lady . . . ?" Clive pointed an accusing finger.

"I'll go and look for it right now, Mr. Palmer."

"Well, hop to it, dear. Chop-chop."

"Okay, five minutes, people," a stage manager called out over the PA system.

"Mom, I'll be right back . . . ," Darkus told Jackie and slid out of the row, jogging down the aisle with a sudden sense of purpose.

"Darkus?" Jackie called after him as he approached the base of the stage.

Clive glanced around anxiously, only to see his stepson waving from below. "Yessssss?" he hissed.

"Er, Clive?" Darkus spoke up. "About your phone . . . I'm no tailor, but judging by the 'bunching' in your jacket enclosure, I think you'll find that—"

"Guess what? I'm no tailor either, but *zip it*. I don't have time for your nonsense, Darkus. Can't you see I'm working? If I'd known you and your mother were going to be this much of a distraction, I wouldn't have given you VIP seating. Debbbbbieeee?" Clive marched offstage.

Darkus sighed and turned to his mother with a shrug. She waved him back to his seat sympathetically as a thundering noise approached the chamber. A dozen security guards unlocked several sets of double doors, ushering in a flood of audience members of all ages and ethnicities: retirees with walking sticks and wheelchairs, young children, even a newborn.

The stampede spread through the auditorium as bodies bumped into each other, clattering into their seats. Darkus examined the rows of eager faces staring at the empty stage. Lights panned and strobed the crowd, which responded with a sea of cell phone screens, held aloft to capture the moment.

Seconds later, the heavily synthesized *Winner's Circle* theme music pumped through the sound system, accompanying a giant graphic of a microphone in a gold halo. The halo exploded into smithereens, coaxing the audience toward a fever pitch. A series of words flashed up on the Jumbotron screens, one after the other: *Talent. Looks. Determination. Who will YOU choose to join . . . The Winner's Circle?*

Then a deep, sonorous voice echoed overhead: "Welcome to week three. Who will enter the circle to win big cash prizes? Who will get *ejected*? Let's hear from our three judges . . ."

An explosion of white light stunned the audience as three figures appeared silhouetted on the stage: a short man with white hair and a blazer; a statuesque woman in a barely there sequined dress; and Clive, striking a pose in his shiny suit, complemented by a dazzling pair of white sneakers. All three judges waved to the audience as the music reached a crescendo. A camera on a crane swung past, taking in the scene.

"Please welcome . . ." The deep voice announced the first two celebrity judges—before reaching Clive.

"And . . . Cliiiiiive Paaaaalmer!"

Clive bowed deeply, almost touching the floor with his nest of hair, which had been expertly coiffed to appear fuller and darker, with a glossy sheen.

"Judges, take your seats."

The judges strode arm in arm down the runway to the panel and took their positions. The music faded, and the audience hushed in anticipation. Just then, a different noise reverberated across the auditorium. It was a phone ringing with the distinctive ringtone of an Italian car horn. The audience murmured in protest. The camera panned across the chamber, looking for the source of the noise.

Clive cranked his head, irate, searching for the culprit, until he realized the ringtone was strangely familiar: in fact, it was his own. His eyebrows arched as he reached into the inside pocket of his suit and pulled out his hitherto missing cell phone. The entire arena fell silent. Not sure what to do, Clive cringed, then answered the call.

"Debbie . . . ? Yes, I've found my phone."

*

Clive stormed through the backstage corridors, accompanied by a director wearing headphones, resting a hand on his shoulder to console him.

"Don't worry, we can edit it out of the repeat," the director suggested.

Clive panted, "It was the most embarrassing moment in over fifteen years of broadcast television."

"Well, to be fair, it wasn't as embarrassing as what happened on *Wheel Spin*," the director added, trying to help. Clive spun, his hackles raised. The director changed tack. "The producers feel it was a very strong show. They told me to say congrats—"

"I want Debbie gone. Fired. Finito," Clive barked.

The director motioned with his hands to calm the situation, until Clive's phone rang again with its distinctive Italian fanfare.

Clive turned to the director. "Can't talk anymore, Keith—"

"It's Ken."

"Ken, Keith, whatever. My agent's on the horn." Clive answered the call. "Yes, Veronique?" A voice rattled through the phone. Clive responded, "A new opportunity?" His face broadened into a jowly grin. "Well, you know me. Show me the monaaayyy."

Clive hung up and pushed through a set of double doors

to find Jackie and Darkus waiting for him in the artists' parking area. His face dropped.

"You, on the other hand, Darkus, you're a bad penny. A bad omen. A bad spark plug. A lemon."

Darkus withstood the verbal bombardment, which he was quite used to.

"Clive!" Jackie reprimanded.

But her husband stood his ground. "That's the last time I have you two here to distract me. Remember: I'm in the winner's circle now, Jax, and I intend to stay there." He waved to his waiting stretch limo. "*Driver?!*"

The limo pulled forward and came to a halt, then the driver tipped his cap, swiftly opening doors for the trio to climb inside.

The limo was warm and quiet, but Darkus's catastrophizer inexplicably began whirring, noting the driver's eyes shifting in the rearview mirror as the engine idled. Jackie sat back in her leather seat and looked out the tinted window. Clive reached for the minibar and sighed.

"Driver, I asked for hummus and pita? Hell-ooo?"

The driver hit the accelerator, and the limo lurched away, causing Clive to spill his drink down his front.

"Ruddy hell! Driver?!"

"Dad . . . ?" Darkus asked.

Clive turned to his stepson, confused. "Huh?"

"Not you," Darkus corrected him. "*Him* . . ." He pointed to the driver, having figured out his true identity.

46

"Sorry about that, Clive," conceded Knightley Senior, removing his disguise and resting the chauffeur's cap on the dashboard. "Hello, Jackie."

"Oh, hello, Alan," she replied, unfazed. "What are you doing here?"

"Yes. What *are* you doing here?" Clive demanded angrily, before adding: "Did you watch the show?"

"I find light entertainment dulls the mind," Knightley responded frankly, then directed his eyes across the rear-view mirror to his son. "Doc, I need to speak to you urgently."

"I already gave you my answer," said Darkus.

"'No' is not an option this time," his father countered.

"What's this all about, Alan?" Jackie asked, sensing something wrong.

Knightley paused, his brow furrowing. "It's about *Bogna* . . ."

The limo turned out of the auditorium gates and fishtailed into the night, its carriage lights vanishing in the fog.

CHAPTER 4
THE SITUATION ROOM

The limo emerged from the mist onto Wolseley Close and parked in the driveway of Clive and Jackie's mock-Tudor house alongside a white Transit van, which was blocking in Clive's new Aston Martin.

"What the hell is *this*?!" Clive yelled at the van as he shimmied between the vehicles.

"The 'Moby Dick,'" replied Darkus, recognizing Uncle Bill's aptly nicknamed mobile command center.

"Well, it's almost touching my Aston!"

Clive opened the front door and stomped upstairs, complaining of a migraine, while Darkus followed his parents into the living room, where Tilly sat cross-legged on the sofa and Uncle Bill erupted from his leather armchair.

"A'right, Doc? Aye, ah've missed ye, laddie." The Scotsman smothered Darkus in a meaty embrace.

"Thanks, Bill. How's the back?" Darkus inquired, in reference to the injury his colleague had sustained on their last case.

"Aye, well, put it this way," said Bill, "I will not be 'twerkin' anytime soon, but ah cannot complain, Doc. Does this mean you're back on the team?" he pleaded.

"We'll see," said Darkus, nodding an awkward greeting to his stepsister before taking a seat at the opposite end of the sofa from her.

Tilly's hair—which was liable to change color at any moment—was currently dyed jet black, indicating the grave circumstances. To his dismay, Darkus noticed she was also wearing a tweed vest.

"Haven't seen you around much," she muttered by way of greeting.

"I hear you've been busy," Darkus answered resentfully. "Nice vest," he added, then addressed the others. "Shall we proceed?"

Knightley Senior drew up a chair to join the huddle. Darkus was reminded of his first mission briefing, in this very room, with his father and Uncle Bill. Those were the good old days, before he knew the sacrifices that being a detective would entail.

In a call to order, Knightley steepled his fingers grimly and started talking. "Yesterday evening our dear friend and trusted employee, Bogna, kept an appointment with a gentleman she met online," he began.

"Really?" said Jackie. "Bogna?"

"She did not return home last night, and we haven't heard from her since," said Knightley. "In fact, her cell phone is switched off. I don't need to tell you this is highly out of character for her."

"Aye," said Uncle Bill anxiously, creaking in his armchair.

"So we're assuming she may have suffered an accident, perhaps amnesia?" Darkus asked with concern, before his slightly rusty detective mind arrived at a more sinister explanation. "Or perhaps she's being held somewhere against her will . . . ," he concluded.

Knightley frowned. "That is our assumption."

Jackie's normally placid face clouded over. Tilly looked to Darkus, concerned. Darkus glanced away, still smarting from the fact that his stepsister had clearly taken his place as his dad's partner in crime-solving. Childish as it might have seemed in the circumstances, Darkus couldn't pretend everything was normal when things were very, very far from normal.

"What do we know about this 'gentleman' she met online?" Darkus asked his father.

Tilly ignored the stepsibling tension and answered for Knightley. "I conducted a cursory search of Bogna's e-mail inbox—approved by Alan, naturally . . ."

Darkus flinched at Tilly using his dad's first name—as if she and "Alan" were old friends or colleagues, instead of acquaintances joined by circumstance, not blood. Still, Darkus maintained a professional attitude and listened.

Tilly continued, "I discovered that Bogna had an account with an online dating site called Hearts of Poland. Here's a printout of her profile picture and online bio." She distributed several pages showing a much younger photo of Bogna standing in a poppy-filled meadow wearing shorts.

Uncle Bill raised his eyebrows and folded the page, tucking it into one of his voluminous inside pockets. "Do go awn, Tilly."

"Under 'likes,' she listed cooking, travel, and long walks on the sidewalk. Under 'dislikes,' she put secrets . . . and bad people."

Knightley nodded somberly and gestured for Tilly to continue.

"She exchanged a few messages with the manager of a restaurant in Hornsey, Marek Pielucha, but we ran some background on him and he checks out. He has a rock-solid alibi: he worked all evening at the restaurant, so he appears to be kosher. The real person of interest is someone named Theo."

Uncle Bill shifted uncomfortably in his seat.

"Theo what?" probed Darkus.

"We don't know yet. His username is 'Theo K.' They exchanged several messages online and planned to speak this week. The Hearts of Poland server is surprisingly robust. I wasn't able to access any of his personal data. Only this . . ."

She passed around a profile printout showing a darkly handsome European man with slicked-back hair and a carefully groomed walrus mustache.

"Well, I suppose she might find him attractive," remarked Jackie.

"I smell a rat," said Knightley.

"Aye, a big 'un," Bill added. "She'd never go for a wally like that."

"I agree. The match is not a convincing one for a number of reasons," Knightley pointed out. "Either this Theo has a very particular type, or . . ."

"Or it's a trap," said Tilly, completing his thought. "With Bogna as bait."

"Set by whom, to catch whom?" said Darkus.

"Set by the Combination, naturally," responded his father, returning to his age-old conspiracy theory. "To catch *us*."

"It's too soon to make that assumption," Darkus suggested, attempting to slow his dad's rush to judgment.

Bill shifted in his seat. "In the past twenty-four hours there's been a rise in chatter between several Combination jimmies, on the phone, text, and e-mail. That would indicate the game is afoot."

"Underwood challenged us to a game," Tilly reminded them. "Maybe this is it. We took one of theirs, now they've taken one of ours."

"Or maybe Bogna just met the man of her dreams," Darkus countered. "Apparently love can cause people to act out of character."

"And you'd know how?" snapped Tilly.

"It's statistically proven," Darkus replied. "Studies suggest that by the time we're of marrying age, over fifty percent of couples will meet online. Bogna must have joined this dating site for a reason."

"And my feminine intuition tells me what it is," said Tilly.

"Proceed," said Darkus.

"Bogna was only going on Internet dates to attract the attention of someone she already knew," Tilly elaborated.

Uncle Bill violently cleared his throat.

Darkus put two and two together. "I see . . ."

"The silly moo," Bill sobbed. "Oh, Boggers." He raised both his chins to the ceiling to address the absent house-keeper. "If ah coulda done things differently, don't ye think I would have done?"

Knightley placed a sympathetic hand on Bill's gigantic shoulder. "Love is a fickle beast."

Jackie raised her eyebrows in bewildered agreement.

"All this banter doesn't change the facts," Tilly advised. "Bogna is missing. Her phone is switched off, and she hasn't made contact with any of us."

Darkus racked his brain. "What about her service provider?"

"We're awaiting records from them," she answered, "which should give us this Theo's number, a call history, text log, and, with luck, a ping from a cell tower to help us triangulate her last known position."

"Has the Met been informed?" said Darkus, referring to the London Metropolitan Police Service.

"Nae," replied Bill. "My department will handle this personally. Whoever scrobbled her will feel the full weecht of the law." The others weren't exactly sure what he'd said, but they got the message. "Whatever the cost," Bill clarified.

However, Darkus knew the Department of the Unexplained was already feeling the impact of far-reaching budget cuts, and a missing housekeeper was hardly going to merit a major government response. And the catastrophizer was humming and rattling at the back of his mind, telling him that Bogna's disappearance, coming only days after the Combination's number-one agent had been apprehended, was too odd to be chance. In the Knowledge—his father's collection of case files, which Darkus had committed to memory—the cardinal rule of any investigation was: never succumb to the luxury of coincidence. Setting aside his increasingly illogical and unruly emotions, Darkus realized that Underwood's arrest and Bogna's disappearance had to be connected. Perhaps his father was right: maybe the Combination had gotten her.

"While we wait for the phone records," Darkus reflected, "Bill, have your men scour surveillance footage in the area of Cherwell Place." He turned to his father and Tilly. "Meanwhile, I suggest you make an appointment at the Hearts of Poland office first thing tomorrow morning and do some old-fashioned detective work. Technology can't always provide the answers we'd like it to."

Tilly shrugged. "It's never let me down."

Darkus frowned at the bad blood between them, knowing that if Bogna was in trouble, she'd need him, his father, and Tilly on the same team—not opposing ones.

"Will you be joining us?" his father asked him, trying hard to disguise the fact that he was begging.

Darkus paused, torn between the detective life he knew, the teenage life he'd tried to know, and the ultimate realization that maybe he didn't know anything at all.

The question mark hanging in the air was supplanted by the two-tone chime of the doorbell—followed by a sharp rap on the front door. All heads turned, fearing the worst. Tilly checked their home surveillance remotely from her phone, which was wirelessly connected to a security camera over the entrance. It showed an image of a burly man waiting impatiently on the welcome mat, picking something out of his teeth. "It's Draycott," she said, identifying the local police inspector who had appointed himself the Knightleys' nemesis.

"I'll handle this," said Knightley Senior. He nodded protectively to Jackie, then strode through the entrance hall and opened the door.

"Interrupting a dysfunctional family gathering, am I . . . ?" whined Draycott.

Knightley glanced over the man's casual attire with disdain: a pastel turtleneck sweater, a pair of permanent-press trousers, and some tassled loafers. "Are you off duty, Inspector, or is this 'casual Friday'?"

"It's *Chief* Inspector. How many times must I remind you?"

Knightley tapped his cranium. "You know me—brain like a sieve. Speaking of which, how's the collapsed lung?"

Draycott winced at the mention of the ill-fated were-wolf hunt on Hampstead Heath that he and Clive had conducted during the Knightleys' last case. "It's *fine*, as a matter of fact." The inspector unconsciously massaged under his left man-boob, which was just visible through his sweater. "The truth is, I popped over to see if Clive— our local celebrity—was free for a capp-u-ccino," he announced, employing the Italian pronunciation. "But my keen powers of observation couldn't help noticing some unusual vehicles in the driveway. As a matter of course, I ran the registration of the white Transit van, and it appears to be *un*registered, which, sadly—for the owner at least—is against the law."

"Don't you have anything better to do?"

"Fighting crime is a twenty-four-seven business, Alan."

"And you're wasting precious time," replied Knightley. "If you had the necessary clearance, you'd know that that license plate is unregistered because it's a *government* plate. SO42. Specialist Operations."

"Then I deduce that your son and that extremely large Scotsman are on the premises?" Draycott pressed him. "Might I ask what you're working on?"

"It's a family affair."

"I like to know everything that goes on in my jurisdiction—*especially* when it relates to *you*." Draycott worked himself up into a lather. "I don't like you, Alan. You're unhinged. Unbalanced. Un*usual*. Wherever you go, trouble follows you like a foul stench."

"Judging by the unmistakable aroma of vinegar and the fleck of haddock between your lower incisors, I deduce the fish-and-chip shop was your last port of call." Knightley offered him a box of toothpicks.

"Oh, verrrry clever, Alan," retorted Draycott, running his tongue over his gums behind his lips in a swift left and right movement.

"Now, if you'll excuse me, we have work to do—" Knightley moved to close the door.

Draycott wedged his loafer in the doorjamb. "Okay, that's obstructing a police officer. I can make life very difficult for you, remember? You and your son left a trail of destruction on your last case: a dead crime boss, several dead animals, a teenage girl with gray hair, not to mention a horribly disfigured classmate, the unfortunate Brendan Doyle. Clive thinks you've recruited his daughter, Matilda, as well. Thick as thieves, you Knightleys. I could call social services right now and press charges of child endangerment, abduction, you name it."

Knightley looked down to find his son had taken his place on the doorstep.

"Chief Inspector," began Darkus, "I must inform you that

you're engaging in malicious prosecution and police harassment. Your actions have been recorded and may be used as evidence. Unless you have reasonable suspicion that a crime has been committed, you have no legal grounds to be here, and I advise you to leave at once."

Draycott's mustache curled. Somewhere upstairs a shower began running, with Clive's enthusiastic but off-key singing above the squeak of the soap.

Tilly joined the Knightleys on the doorstep in a show of unity. "Party's over, Inspector."

"It's *Chief* Inspector," moaned Draycott as the door closed in his face.

Knightley Senior stood in the entrance hall and took a moment to admire the two awkward-looking teenagers standing before him. "Darkus . . . Tilly . . . ?" he ventured. "Will you return to London and stay at the office in order to facilitate an early start?"

Knightley gazed at his son with a longing that even twenty-odd years of detective work couldn't disguise. Darkus glanced at the imaginary question mark still hanging in the air and realized that, for once, Draycott was right: he and his father *were* thick as thieves—and right now they had to remain thicker and closer than ever.

"It is logical," Darkus conceded.

"Sure," said Tilly, seeing her own father appear on the stairs in a bathrobe and towel turban. "I'd rather be anywhere than here."

"Fine with me," said Clive and flounced off into the bedroom.

Jackie appeared from the living room, with Uncle Bill shifting on his feet in the background. Knightley silently turned to his former wife, awaiting her permission.

"Bogna is family," she admitted. "I trust you, Alan," she went on, weighing it up in her head. "You've never let any harm come to them . . . *yet*."

"I'd give my own life first," he replied with complete sincerity.

"Aye, and ah'd take a bullet for 'em. Possibly even a grenade," Bill added, although it didn't sound as reassuring as he intended.

Jackie examined Darkus, then Tilly, and then nodded. "Phones on. I want updates. Hourly," she insisted. She fixed her gaze on Knightley. "Alan, how are you going to manage without Bogna? Who's going to make your sandwiches the way you both like them?"

"I'll manage," he answered. "I've managed in the past."

"I remember your cooking skills," she said with a hint of a smile.

Knightley shrugged. "No one died. And I've improved a little since then."

"If I can be of any assistance, I'm always at the end of the phone," she offered. "I mean it." Her eyes brightened for an instant.

Knightley's cheeks appeared to redden slightly. Uncle

Bill peeked up from under the brim of his homburg hat.

"Thanks, Jax," Knightley replied. "Me too. I promise." He picked up his tweed overcoat and slung it on, propping his tweed walking hat on his head. "The game is, most definitely, afoot."

Darkus watched the fleeting moment between his parents evaporate, then followed his father, Tilly, and Uncle Bill through the front door to the waiting Transit van.

"Wait a second, Dad," he said, turning back to the house.

Darkus climbed the stairs and crossed the landing to his bedroom. He opened the door and walked with purpose to the closet. He inched it open and saw his Donegal tweed overcoat hanging there, wrapped in see-through plastic. Beside it was a three-piece tweed suit with a pair of polished brogues waiting below. He gathered up his clothes, along with the secure cell phone Uncle Bill had given him, his lock pick set, and the jeweler's loupe that served as a magnifying glass. Darkus closed the closet door and left without looking back.

CHAPTER 5
PRELUDE TO A CASE

Uncle Bill drove them to London, through the warren of backstreets that made up the borough of Islington, past forgotten warehouses and railway tracks, until they reached the familiar curving row of terraced houses signposted *Cherwell Place*.

Knightley led Darkus and Tilly into number 27 while Uncle Bill decided to sleep in the van, claiming it would be "too quiet" in the office without Bogna present—and agreeing it would be wrong to take advantage of her empty bed. Besides, Darkus had already begun sweeping the housekeeper's room for potential clues, which would have been considerably more challenging with a gigantic and somewhat weepy Scotsman occupying it.

Finding nothing of immediate interest to the investigation, Darkus and Tilly made up their respective beds in the office and on the landing. Knightley Senior arrived with a tray of milk and some jam sandwiches—triangles, not squares, of course—but that was where the similarity ended. The triangles were uneven, and Darkus suspected his father had used relish instead of jam.

After Knightley exited, Tilly pushed her plate aside in disgust. "I can't eat this."

Darkus finished his round out of duty, reluctantly swallowing the last bite before replying, "He's doing his best, I suppose."

Tilly nodded. "I guess you can't choose your parents," she sighed. "And you can't choose what happens to them," she added, directing her eyes to her smartphone screen.

Darkus knew she was referring to her mother's death: the car accident in the ice storm; the event that shaped her entire being.

"Dad mentioned the hard drive you found," he explained, unsure what her reaction would be.

Tilly held up her phone to show a timer counting down from seventy-six hours, decreasing in minutes, seconds, and hundredths of seconds. "That's the estimated time it'll take to decrypt the files and find out what kind of game Underwood's really playing."

"And you believe Bogna's disappearance has something to do with it?"

"I do," said Tilly soberly. "I've got my best contacts working on it around the clock at a secure online location. With any luck, it'll deliver us the Combination on a plate, served cold—along with the names of the people responsible for leaving me alone in the world, with nothing but a third-rate TV personality for a dad."

Darkus nodded, thanking heaven on a daily basis that Clive was only a stepfather—and an absentee one at that.

"But I wouldn't say you have nothing," he countered, choosing his next words carefully. "I mean, you can't choose your stepsiblings either," he observed. "But I'm very grateful to have you."

Tilly blushed, momentarily lost for words. "Thanks, Doc."

"Don't mention it. Here's to friendship," said Darkus, raising his glass of milk and clinking it with hers. "Now, my dear Tilly, we have a missing person to find."

The pair sniffed their respective glasses to make sure the milk was within its sell-by date, then drained them and got to work, falling into the familiar patter of long-standing detective colleagues. The plan came together quickly—but the execution would be anyone's guess.

CHAPTER 6
A PERFECT MATCH

Uncle Bill mopped his perspiring brow, sucked the dregs of his stogie, and stubbed it out, then appeared to wobble on his feet, complaining of a lack of sleep, a lack of chocolate digestives, and a heavy heart. Darkus and Tilly supported him as best they could upon entering the depressingly colorful lobby of the office building. The trio approached the reception desk, which was decorated with giant pink and red heart shapes.

"We're the Billochs," Darkus informed the female receptionist. "I'm Darren, and this is my sister, Tracy," he added, pointing at Tilly. Fortunately the matching tweed outfits added to the deception nicely. "We have an appointment with Hearts of Poland. Right, Pa?" Darkus looked up in concern at Uncle Bill, who was now sweating profusely and seemed to have forgotten his vital role in the operation. The best-laid plans could fall apart due to human error—and Bill was riddled with those.

"Aye, son," Bill finally replied, doffing his hat toward the receptionist. "Ah'd like to find a wife-slash-mammy for these two malinkies."

The receptionist shuffled her mouse, checked her computer screen for a few moments, then replied, "One of our experienced matchmakers will see you shortly."

After Bill had completed a folder of paperwork, a thin Eastern European woman with bleached hair and near-perfect English ushered them into her office. The walls were decorated with photos of smiling couples, some holding champagne glasses, others wearing wedding outfits—obviously all successful matches. Bill wheezed, squeezing himself into a plastic chair alongside his two "kids."

"It's very unusual to bring children to a consultation," she began.

"We feel we can help Dad make an informed decision," said Darkus.

The matchmaker raised her eyebrows before returning her attention to Bill.

"Well, let's begin by telling me a little about what you're looking for in a partner."

"Well, she must be Polish, of course," said Bill.

"Is there any reason for this?" asked the matchmaker.

"Force o' habit," replied Bill.

"I see. And what else can you tell me about your dream woman?"

"She's got to be a big lass. I don't go for shrinkin' violets or Gloria's Secret models."

Tilly elbowed Bill somewhere in the rib area, keeping him on message.

"Preferably a good cook and a whiz with a vacuum cleaner to boot," Bill added.

"That image is a little . . . old-fashioned, don't you think?" asked the matchmaker.

"Aye, she is a wee bit old-fashioned. That's why ah love her."

The matchmaker's face softened a little. "It's almost as if you can already see her, right there in your mind's eye."

"Aye, I can. Ah cannot get her *out* of mah mind's eye."

"How romantic . . ."

"She's like a munchy box, with a roll 'n' pie and a plate o' clapshot."

"I beg your pardon?"

Tilly nudged him in the rib area again.

"Never mind, lassie."

"Well, we do have one lady who fits that description," advised the matchmaker. "Her name is Bogna Rejesz."

Bill winced and inflated his cheeks. "Aye, that's a bonny name," he managed.

"She's employed as a housekeeper in North London," the matchmaker went on.

"She sounds nice," added Darkus.

"Yeah," Tilly chimed in.

The matchmaker pursed her lips. "I must advise you not to get your hopes up. Miss Rejesz has already been on a successful date with another Hearts of Poland member."

Darkus and Tilly looked to Uncle Bill, who had turned a fiery red color and unconsciously crumpled his homburg hat in his immense, pudgy hands. Darkus feared steam, or even cigar smoke, could erupt from the Scotsman's ears at any moment.

"What's the name of the person she went on a date with?" Darkus asked delicately.

"I'm afraid that would be a breach of our client-confidentiality rules. All our members' personal details are kept safe and sound in the file room . . ." She gestured through the wall in the direction of the corridor.

"Why, that ba'-heid—!" Bill lurched to his feet, until Darkus and Tilly forcibly pushed him into his seat again.

"Calm down, Dad," counseled Darkus.

"He's very passionate . . . ," Tilly explained. "Ever since Mom passed away, things haven't been easy for us."

Darkus flinched at his stepsister's commitment to the cover story: this small detail was so close to home that it must have cut her to the bone, but she didn't show it a bit.

"I see," said the matchmaker sympathetically.

"Perhaps it would be better if Tracy and I stretched our legs?" said Darkus. "Right, Pa?"

"Aye," whimpered Bill, then pulled out a hankie and blew his nose with the force of a category-five hurricane.

*

Moments later, Darkus and Tilly had exited the match-maker's office and were making their way up the corridor in the direction of the file room. They smiled innocently at a young male assistant sitting at a computer, attempting to match lonely hearts' profiles on his desktop.

"Can I help you?" he asked with an Eastern European accent.

"We're just giving Dad some space," replied Tilly.

"Of course. The fridge is up the corridor if you want some snack."

Tilly followed Darkus as he glanced at the doors to the kitchen and the bathroom, before arriving at an unmarked door with a mortise lock. Darkus slipped on his gloves and opened his set of lock picks, but Tilly simply pushed the door open, finding it unlocked. Darkus shrugged and followed her inside.

"We're in," Darkus spoke into a small flesh-colored earpiece, wirelessly connected to his secure phone.

His father's voice returned through the earpiece: "Good."

The file room was extensive and well organized. Darkus and Tilly converged on the heavy metal filing cabinet marked K. Tilly reached out eagerly with her unprotected fingers, until Darkus stopped her with a gloved hand.

"Prints," he whispered and slowly opened the drawer.

68

She might have been a partner in the family business, but she still had a few things to learn.

Darkus and Tilly stood on tiptoe to peer inside. Darkus leafed through the files until he reached "Theo K."

"Bingo," he muttered, removing the file and confirming the image of the handsome, mustachioed man in the profile picture.

Darkus began speed-reading the contents while Tilly photographed them with her smartphone. Then Darkus stopped.

"The suspect's name is Theodore Kojak," he whispered into his earpiece.

"What?" Knightley crackled back.

"Who's that?" asked Tilly.

"It's clearly an assumed name," Darkus explained. "Theodore Kojak is the name of a fictional TV detective with a penchant for lollipops, made famous by the actor Telly Savalas."

"Correct." Knightley sounded even more concerned. "It's so obviously an assumed name that it's either the work of a complete amateur . . ."

"Or it's part of the game. A trap," concluded Tilly.

"In which case, the Combination is alive and well," declared Knightley.

"Even though Underwood is locked in a self-imposed hypnotic state in the secure ward of Broadmoor Hospital?" argued Darkus.

"Then perhaps there's a new player in charge," his father replied.

Darkus and Tilly waved good-bye to the matchmaker, who handed Bill another wad of tissues and gave him a hug before ushering him out of the lobby. Darkus hailed a black cab, and Knightley's Fairway taxi pulled right up to collect them. Once inside, Knightley pressed the intercom to speak to them from the driver's seat.

"What've we got?" His voice entered the cabin.

"Mah heart feels like it's been flushed right down the cludgie," said Bill, wiping his nose.

Tilly didn't look up from her smartphone. "I just ran a check on the suspect's address. It doesn't exist."

"So his name's fake and his address is fake," moaned Knightley.

"And so is his pose," said Darkus, examining the photo closely. "I don't know how I could've missed this the first time; I must be getting long in the tooth. There's something about this photograph—the warm lighting, the soft focus, the careful use of Photoshop—that makes me think he's a professional."

"A professional what?" asked Tilly.

"A professional *actor*," replied Darkus. "This is a 'head shot,' commonly used by actors for the procurement of work. Judging by the theatricality of his appearance, the absurdity of his assumed name—not to mention his mustache—I'd hazard a guess he's a star of stage and perhaps the small screen. I refer, of course, to TV."

"Sound reasoning, Doc," said his father through the intercom.

"Tilly, I suggest you compare that photo against every acting agency database in London," Darkus went on. "I suspect we'll have our man sooner than you think. Only this time he'll be auditioning for the role of kidnapper."

Tilly nodded, quietly impressed, before continuing the search on her smartphone.

"Chalk that one up to old-fashioned detective work," Darkus added.

"We haven't found her yet . . . ," she reminded him.

By noon, Tilly had a photo match for the suspect, whose real name was Humphrey Sturgess, a character actor from Kent who had appeared in a handful of TV detective dramas, and more recently played the villain in a local community theater. The waxed walrus mustache was apparently his trademark.

By 1 p.m. the team had arrived to interview Sturgess's representatives, Scene Stealers, a little-known talent agency located on the top floor of a seedy tenement in London's Soho district. Uncle Bill examined the tall staircase and decided his time was better spent watching the car and keeping an eye on the parade of colorful characters entering and leaving the building.

Reaching the cramped office at the summit of the building, Darkus wasted no breath on small talk. Regardless of who was behind this, the first forty-eight hours of any missing-persons investigation were the most critical; and this missing person was someone very close to their hearts. "We believe your client, one Humphrey Sturgess, is a person of interest in a kidnapping," Darkus began.

The pasty, middle-aged man with a comb-over and a cheap blue suit (who was the managing director and sole employee of Scene Stealers) made no attempt to evade the question.

"Ah, I thought it was all a bit too good to be true," the man admitted. "When it came to regular acting jobs, Humphrey couldn't get arrested—if you'll excuse the pun."

"Excused," said Darkus.

"For a leading man, Humph didn't have that je ne sais quoi. And then there was the mustache." The agent frowned and shook his head. "Anyway, a few weeks ago I got a call from a production company I'd never heard of called Clorr Entertainment. They said they were looking for someone to play a part in a reality show. The job involved pretending to be a client on an Internet dating site. Humphrey had to play a Pole. His accent was okay and he could turn on the charm, for a price. He had to play along, go on a date with a female contestant, and the film crew would all be there in secret—behind mirrors, in vans, that kind of thing. Then he was supposed to woo the woman in question and take her on a trip to America."

"America?" Tilly snapped.

"Yes, America," the man repeated.

Darkus looked to his father in surprise, then returned his steely gaze to the agent. "Proceed."

"Well, the company offered to pay for the flights, room and board, even a midsized rental car with comprehensive insurance. Now I'd call that star treatment. All Humph had to do was make sure the contestant reached America in one piece. On top of the dough, they also promised him a big audition for the lead in a Hollywood movie when he got there. As you can imagine, the whole thing was too good to turn down."

Darkus cut in. "So I assume they were planning to fly to Los Angeles, California, the home of the movie business?"

"Exact-a-mundo. Funny thing was, though—they were one-way flights, not round-trip." The agent shrugged, baffled.

The detectives looked at one another, more concerned than ever.

"When were the flights booked for?" demanded Knightley.

"They would've departed from Heathrow yesterday afternoon," the man answered, re-combing his hair. "Around three p.m."

Both Knightleys unconsciously checked their wristwatches in unison, calculating the relative time zones

(British Summer Time versus Pacific Time), before looking up, equally perplexed.

"That means they've already landed in the US," said Tilly, beating them to it.

"We've lost them . . . ," Knightley groaned.

"Not necessarily." Darkus drummed his fingers on the agent's desk. "I need to see all correspondence between you and Clorr Entertainment. I want numbers, e-mails, anything you've got. I warn you, this is now an official police matter, and your reputation in the entertainment industry—which I fear is not stellar—is currently at stake."

"I'll work with you any way I can," replied the agent. "And by the way, would either of you two youngsters be interested in doing commercials? I love your look. Especially the tweed."

CHAPTER 7
DUTY FREE

Events were moving rapidly, and logic had to move at an equal pace. Darkus and Tilly had both been schooled in detective work by Knightley Senior: Darkus by reading his dad's journals, known as the Knowledge; Tilly with on-the-job training over the past several months. That schooling involved a variety of techniques, such as: always make a mental note of every person and/or object in a room, in case it becomes evidence; always sit at the back of any café, restaurant, or place of business, in order to observe and cover all exits; always carry a magnifying glass, a jeweler's loupe, or a smartphone macro lens; and finally—and most significantly in this case—*always carry your passport.* Knightley Senior's reasoning was that no matter where you are, you never know when immediate flight from the country, by plane, train, or boat, might be necessary—or even vital—to a case. And besides, should some terrible accident (or worse) befall you, a passport is the most reliable and widely accepted form of identification. For this reason, both Darkus and Tilly were in possession of their passports, as was Knightley. Uncle Bill, on the other hand, couldn't remember where his was.

"Ah think it's in mah ski jacket, but I don't remember where ah put that," he complained from the backseat of the cab, sandwiched between Darkus and Tilly. "In any case, ah've booked ye three on the next flight to Los Angeles, departing at fifteen hundred hours on Virgin Atlantic. Yer tickets an' travel papers are all arranged, an' ye'll be fast-tracked through security, no questions asked. Ah'll follow ye as soon as we get some background on this Clorr Entertainment and the results of the security camera invest-igation. So far, all we have is this . . ." Bill looked like he'd bitten down on a lemon as he held up a tablet PC displaying Heathrow Airport surveillance footage, time-stamped the previous day.

On the screen, Bogna could be seen wandering dreamily through airport security, escorted by the mustachioed Humphrey Sturgess. Both were dressed for a vacation: Sturgess in baggy harem pants and Bogna in shorts, a T-shirt, and a large sun hat.

"Looks like she might have been under the influence," observed Darkus.

"The influence of what, though . . . ?" said Tilly.

"Alcohol, or possibly a sleeping pill," he replied.

Bill puffed out his cheeks. "If ah get mah hands on that chanty wrassler . . ."

76

Knightley nodded soberly from the driver's seat. "Try to remain calm, Bill. Look after Bessie for me."

Darkus looked confused, until he realized his dad was referring to the car.

The black cab pulled up behind a row of taxis at the drop-off area outside Heathrow Airport's Terminal 3. Darkus and Tilly stepped out with only a backpack between them, and were immediately surrounded by travelers wheeling luggage and pushing heavy carts. Knightley handed the car keys to Uncle Bill, who spontaneously grabbed his colleague in a crushing embrace.

"Oh, Alan."

"We'll find her," Knightley assured him. "You have my word."

"If anyone can, ye and Darkus can," Bill choked, then straightened up into a salute, fixing the homburg hat on his head. He then pulled the two teenagers into his bulging midriff.

They said their good-byes, and Uncle Bill got behind the wheel of the cab, accidentally blew the horn, activated the windshield wipers, flicked on the orange *For Hire* sign, then screeched away from the curb.

Darkus and Tilly followed Knightley as he strode through the automatic glass doors, then paused in front of the flashing departures board. Knightley's ears seemed to lift, and his eyes gazed off into the scatter of flight numbers. Darkus looked up at his father apprehensively.

"You okay, Dad?"

"I'm getting one of my feelings, Doc. The feeling that all is not right. Perhaps it's part of the game . . ."

"Maybe you shouldn't look at the numbers for too long. You know what can happen . . . ," Darkus warned, remembering that his father could slip back into a narcoleptic trance given the slightest opportunity. Underwood's hypnotic powers had left a lasting scar on his dad's subconscious, but Darkus needed his father alert and responsive for this very personal and soon-to-be foreign investigation.

"Alan?" a female voice interrupted him. It was Miss Khan—Darkus and Tilly's science teacher from Cranston School, who now doubled as their technical adviser. She nodded respectfully, lowered her headscarf, and flipped her jet-black ponytail over her shoulder. "I came as soon as I could."

The Knightleys turned to Tilly, who shrugged. "I figured we'd need more than a few travel adapters on this job."

"Hello, Aaeesha," said Knightley, using Miss Khan's little-known and even less-used first name. "I haven't seen you since the parent-teacher evening."

Miss Khan nodded prudently. "I'm glad you were there. I hope things are improving at home," she said, looking from him to Darkus and back again.

"Well, we're here sharing some male bonding time, aren't we, son? The only way we know how."

"You could say that," answered Darkus.

"What've you got for us, Miss Khan?" said Tilly, getting down to business.

Miss Khan led the trio to a seating area and surreptitiously reached into her handbag. First she took out a junior-sized electric shaver and handed it to Darkus.

"Well, in fact, I don't require that just yet," Darkus admitted, self-consciously rubbing his hairless chin.

"It's no ordinary shaver," the science teacher explained. "It's an EMP device. That's an electromagnetic pulse, to you and me."

Knightley turned to Tilly. "Translation, please?"

"It interferes with machines," began Tilly. "Blasts them with radio waves that incapacitate their circuitry and render them useless. It can stop a phone, a car, even an incoming missile. Obviously you shouldn't attempt your first shave on the plane."

"I don't intend to," answered Darkus.

"Next," said Miss Khan, reaching deeper into her handbag and pulling out a compact hairdryer. Tilly's eyes lit up. "It's a perfectly adequate blow-dryer," Miss Khan went on. "But it also doubles as a blow*torch* . . . This is the gas reservoir. If you press this selector button all the way, it will emit a fine gas flame that will melt steel, a door lock, what have you."

The Knightleys both glanced at Tilly's hair, concerned.

"I'd advise you not to do your hair on the plane either," said Darkus.

"Funny," she responded, deadpan.

Knightley waited his turn, watching with anticipation.

"And for the man who has everything . . ." Miss Khan produced a small silver medallion on a chain, passing it to the elder detective.

"Does it strangle people?" inquired Darkus.

"No, it protects them," she replied. "It's a Saint Christopher medal, the patron saint of travelers."

"I didn't know you were religious," Knightley murmured. "Or superstitious?"

"It belonged to my father," she answered. "Bring it back in one piece."

Knightley examined the small silver disc, with the engraving around the edge: *Saint Christopher Protect Us.* "Thank you," he responded, carefully coiling the necklace around his fingers and sliding it into his top pocket.

"Good luck, Alan." Miss Khan grabbed the two teens around the shoulders. "Same goes for you two. And don't forget your assignments over the summer break." She returned to her default role of schoolteacher. "I'll see you in September, safe and sound, with your homework completed." She nodded to Knightley, as if indicating that he should take care of himself and, more important, his two young charges.

"Will do," said Tilly, throwing a salute.

Darkus watched the science teacher raise her headscarf and walk away in the direction of the train platforms. "What about Mom?" he questioned his dad.

"Hmm," said Knightley, absently tapping his nose.

Darkus was no stranger to body language, and deduced exactly what his father was thinking: *Mum's the word.*

"Well?" Darkus asked anyway.

His father stared at the departures board, losing himself in the flashing numbers again. "If we're playing a game with the Combination, which I am quite certain we are—"

"Though we don't have conclusive evidence of that yet," Darkus interjected.

"For once, Doc, I'd ask you to trust my judgment. *If* the Combination is the orchestrator of this peculiar problem we face, it is essential that we compartmentalize your mother, and more important—given his fragile history— your stepfather, Clive. For their own safety."

"By compartmentalize you mean . . . ?"

"Maintain plausible deniability."

"In other words . . . ?"

"Don't tell them a thing," instructed Knightley.

"Why didn't you just say that?" said Tilly, doing a panoramic eye roll.

"Don't worry, Doc," his father assured him. "I'll take full responsibility. Now, once we've checked in, we have an hour before we're required to be at the gate. I, for one, feel the need for some retail therapy."

Tilly's face lit up. "Me too!"

*

"Are you sure we can afford all this, Dad?" asked Darkus as the trio emerged from three separate changing rooms, each outfitted in khaki-colored cotton shirts and linen shorts, sporting a distinctly tropical flair.

The trip through security had been uneventful, and Miss Khan's gadgets had not set off any alarm bells. Now Knightley Senior seemed determined to enjoy himself.

"Money's for spending, Doc. And I haven't seen the sun since long before my 'episode.'"

"Well, I don't care if you can afford it or not," said Tilly. "I'm liking my style." She put on a pair of big sunglasses and struck a pose in the mirror.

The Knightleys adjusted their safari jackets and stared down at their exposed white legs.

"Well, it's not exactly our natural state . . . ," Knightley admitted, as they squinted, examining themselves in the mirror. "But I think we could pass for natives."

"California is a hot and arid climate, so obviously tweed is out of the question," observed Darkus. "However, with the use of a reasonably high-factor sunscreen, I believe we'll blend in within a few days. British tourists are usually given away by their refusal to remove their tank tops or to wear sunscreen, hence their tendency to go bright red, creating what's known as a 'lobster tan,'" he explained.

"Good point, Doc," his father concurred.

Tilly looked at the pair of them and shook her head.

Knightley called over to the sales assistant, "We'll take one complete outfit in every color you've got. And don't worry about wrapping them."

After visiting an expensive luggage shop, the three travelers packed their new belongings into three carry-on wheelie bags and made the trek to the departure gate. Darkus remained mystified by his father's unexpected fit of vacation spirit, but put it down to nerves regarding what might await them on the other side of the pond—American slang for the Atlantic Ocean. It was now approaching forty-eight hours with no contact from Bogna. Her behavior in the surveillance footage was inexplicable, and her ultimate role in the mystery equally so.

The other problem weighing on his mind was: why America? To get them off their home turf? To dazzle them with freedom, justice, and supersize fries? Or to lure them into a trap five thousand miles from their natural habitat? One thing Darkus did know was that if Bogna was bait of some kind, then they were taking it: hook, line, and sinker.

As they approached the gate, passing the row of hulking Boeings beyond the glass, Knightley had one last embarrassment in store for Darkus on British soil.

"I wonder if you could help us," Knightley asked the uniformed woman in red behind the airline departure counter. "The kids have suffered a terrible shock, losing someone very close to them, and I wondered if it wouldn't be too much trouble . . . to upgrade us. They're taking it really hard," he added.

"We don't have any seats in Premium Economy," the woman in red responded, before breaking a smile. "But we do have three in Upper Class."

"Outstanding."

CHAPTER 8
FLIGHT PLAN

The Knightleys and Tilly settled into their seats across from one another at the front of the plane, experimenting with the fold-down flat beds and the entertainment systems. Knightley Senior sipped a glass of champagne and fastened his seat belt tightly across his waist.

Darkus browsed a selection of movies before switching off the screen in order to focus his mind on the facts: Bogna was missing, having fallen victim to a honey trap performed by a professional actor and engineered by the mysterious Clorr Entertainment, who had conspired to spirit the unfortunate housekeeper to the United States. Darkus used the onboard Wi-Fi to conduct a brief investigation of Clorr Entertainment, but all its employees had automatic out-of-office replies, its owners were untraceable, and its addresses, real and online, were currently "under construction." All this while Underwood lay unconscious in a secure hospital ward. Darkus found the wheels of his deductive mind spinning hopelessly, lacking the connective tissue to gain traction. He turned to

Tilly and found her staring at her phone, watching the timer counting down: 61:45:03—2—1 . . .

"Any update?" he asked.

"A few fragments of e-mails. Nothing about who the Combination are or where I can find them. Nothing more about the murder." The mention of her mother's death brought a ghostly pall over Tilly's face. "Nothing relevant. They'll ping me when the drive is readable."

"If you want my assistance, I'm all ears."

"I'll let you know when I'm ready to share," she said, toying with her sunglasses. "You know, your dad's all right. Weird . . . but all right."

The aircraft nudged back from the terminal gate and taxied across the byways toward its designated runway.

Knightley Senior shifted anxiously in his seat as the jet engines droned to life. He leaned across the aisle to the others. "I understand neither of you have traveled to the States before, so when we disembark in Los Angeles, meaning 'City of Angels'—also known as LA for short—I'll ask you, for once in your lives, to follow my lead. The thing about America is, everything's bigger. The cars, the characters . . . especially the sandwiches. And I can't promise they'll be triangles and not squares. But we'll survive. And we will find Bogna, mark my words."

"The trail will be cold," replied Darkus. "How are we supposed to navigate a foreign city?"

"Every investigation is like a foreign city, Doc. We simply

read the clues and make our deductions, just as we do on home soil . . . Trust me."

The bulbous engines on either side of the fuselage reached a deafening whine as the massive aircraft accelerated to full tilt, pinning the trio in their seats.

Knightley slipped the chain of the Saint Christopher medal around his neck, then gripped the seat with both hands as the g-forces took effect.

The ground fell away, the highways and buildings were reduced to toddler toys, and the plane passed through the cloud layer and into the flat blue sky, approaching cruising altitude.

Darkus turned to his father, whose eyes were clamped shut, his nostrils flared and his nose whistling with every inhale and exhale.

"Dad?" Darkus whispered. "Dad . . . ?"

His father appeared to be unconscious.

Tilly turned her attention away from the window. "Is he . . . ? Has he . . . ?"

"I thought this might happen," Darkus sighed, reaching over to check his father's pulse, which confirmed that his dad was experiencing one of his "episodes": a narcoleptic trance, brought on by stress. "Mom said he never was a good flyer."

In what had become a regular occurrence, Darkus found himself without a supervising adult. He felt the familiar sick feeling in his stomach, and hoped his father's lapse would be shorter than previous ones. He explained the unusual condition to the flight crew, who set aside his father's meals in case he woke from his trance at some point during the twelve-hour flight. Tilly busied herself with coding on her smartphone, while Darkus set his wristwatch to show Los Angeles local time, which was eight hours behind British Summer Time. Then he tried to set his body clock by settling down for some sleep. Whether his dad was a working partner or not, Darkus would require all his mental powers for this case.

As the plane followed its course, the sky appeared to bend, following the curvature of the earth. Darkus drifted in and out of consciousness, first finding Tilly on her smartphone, then halfway through a Hollywood action movie, then curled up under a blanket, dead to the world. Knightley Senior continued to breathe heavily, oblivious to changing continents and time zones, wrapped in a duvet by a flight attendant, unconscious but still sitting bolt upright.

Darkus stretched his legs a few times, knowing from his research that it was the best defense against deep vein thrombosis, or blood clots: a common problem among long-haul flyers. He also flexed his father's legs for him, as he'd seen the nurses do so many times during Knightley's four-year coma state. For comfort, the flight attendant had replaced his dad's brogues with a pair of red slippers.

What Darkus didn't notice was a teenage boy sitting a

few rows behind him, dressed casually in sunglasses, head-phones, and a baseball cap pulled low to obscure his face—but watching Darkus and Tilly's every move and tapping notes into his smartphone.

Darkus was woken by the flight staff raising the shades on the windows. He leaned up and looked out at a blazing orange sunset, glaring down over a range of dusty hills dotted with palm trees, white houses, and mansions. Below the hills was a layer of soupy-looking smog, similar to what he imagined lurking in the streets of London in Victorian times. Only this smog didn't creep around gaslights and hansom cabs; it crept around a cluster of glass-clad skyscrapers that reflected the hard desert light, surrounded by a seemingly endless sprawl of low-lying homes stretching in all directions. The streets were arranged in a near perfect grid, overlaid with a tangled web of ten-lane freeways, full to capacity with gleaming cars, trucks, and semi-trailers. Darkus recognized the landmarks: the funnel-shaped Capitol Records building with the needle pointing upward; the familiar letters of the Hollywood sign propped on a hillside.

But the overwhelming thought on Darkus's mind was: how on earth would they find Bogna in a city of this magnitude?

The captain's voice arrived over the PA system: "We're

beginning our descent into LA. The local time is just after 7:05 p.m. It's currently a balmy twenty-seven degrees— that's eighty-one Fahrenheit—with a *combination* of gentle winds and a coastal marine layer to the west . . ."

Knightley Senior stirred, his arms jolting to life. "The Co—the Cohhhhm—the Combination!" His eyes popped open, taking in his surroundings. "Doc?" he blurted. "Where am I? And why am I wearing these ungodly slippers?"

"It's okay, Dad, we're about to land in Los Angeles," said Darkus. "I'm really glad you're back," he confessed.

Knightley smiled, looking around, bleary-eyed. "These seats really are comfortable. I slept like a log."

The plane performed a textbook landing, and ten minutes later the trio exited onto a jet bridge leading to the Bradley Terminal of Los Angeles International Airport. Darkus felt the wave of California heat through the gangway as they passed into a glass corridor, following the signs to Immigration and Customs, then descended an escalator under an American flag and a smiling photo of the president of the United States.

"He still owes me one," Knightley muttered. But, even after consulting the Knowledge that was stored in his head, Darkus had no idea which case he was referring to.

They joined a line that snaked around several rows of barrier posts, then approached a glass cubicle containing a stern-looking immigration officer. The three of them presented their passports and the travel papers supplied by Uncle Bill.

"What's the purpose of your visit?" asked the officer.

"To find an old friend," replied Knightley.

The officer looked them over for a few moments, then abruptly stamped their passports in quick succession and waved them through.

Having beaten them through the lines, the teenage boy in the baseball cap, headphones, and sunglasses observed their movements from the baggage carousel, unnoticed.

The Knightleys and Tilly loaded their carry-on luggage onto a cart and wheeled it through customs without delay, entering the main concourse. The teenager in the baseball cap walked briskly ahead, whispered something to a representative at a car rental desk, then vanished through the automatic doors into the gathering dusk.

Knightley Senior took the lead, scanning the rental kiosks until he saw a slightly sweaty man in a white shirt, sporting a goatee beard and holding a misspelled sign that read *Knightly*.

The trio approached the man cautiously.

"The Knightleys?" asked the man enthusiastically. "I'm Todd. I'll be your greeter."

"Greeter?" asked Darkus.

"It's an American thing," Knightley explained privately. "He will escort us to our vehicle, engage us in light chit-chat, and then wait until we give him a tip."

Darkus turned to Tilly. "Dad means a gratuity on top of the agreed cost of service."

"I know what he means," she snapped, then turned to the greeter. "Who sent you?" she demanded.

"A company called . . ." The greeter checked his paperwork. "SO42?"

"Bill thought of everything. Lead on, Todd," said Knightley and gave him the cart to push. "It's very important to tip everyone you meet," the detective carried on to his colleagues. "That's why I have a stash of one-dollar bills in my 'fanny pack.'"

"Your what?" Darkus and Tilly said in unison.

"It's what we call a 'bum bag,'" Knightley responded and took a bunch of bills out from the nylon bag belted around his waist.

The greeter led them out to the curb, past an array of travelers, SUVs, yellow taxis, and a handful of paparazzi pursuing a celebrity; then across a busy access road to a parking lot where a large, shiny Dodge sedan waited for them. Darkus wasn't a car fanatic, but even he experienced a shiver of pleasure at the sight of the gleaming machine.

"This is your vehicle," said Todd grandly. "It must be your lucky day, because they've given you a complimentary upgrade. A midsize sedan for the price of a compact."

"What he means is—" began Darkus.

"I get it," replied Tilly.

"With collision insurance included, and less than a

hundred miles on the clock," Todd announced proudly. "The GPS is built in; just press this button here . . . And you're ready to roll."

Todd loitered by the driver's-side door until Knightley handed over a sheaf of one-dollar bills.

"Thank you, sir, and welcome to Los Angeles." The greeter handed over the key fob, pocketed the money, and returned to the terminal.

"So where are we going?" asked Tilly.

"Has Bill organized a hotel?" asked Darkus.

Knightley took some paperwork from his fanny pack. "The Mar Vista Motor Inn," he read out. "It doesn't sound encouraging."

"I'd better have my own room," Tilly demanded. "With a hot tub."

"Don't get your hopes up," advised Knightley, examining the dashboard.

"Shotgun," called Tilly.

The Knightleys spun around. "Where?"

"I'm *riding* shotgun," she explained, shaking her head as she hopped into the car. "That means I'm taking the front passenger seat, you doofus," she lectured Knightley. "See, you learn something new every day. And the ignition is *here*." She pointed to a "Start" button.

Darkus took the backseat, which was the size of a small bed.

Knightley pressed the button, causing the engine and

lights to flick on. "Now, we're all a little jet-lagged, and as our designated driver, I need to keep my wits about me." He tried to enter the address into the GPS until Tilly nudged him aside and entered it for him.

The GPS began speaking in an automated American voice. "Please pro-ceed to the highlighted route . . ."

Knightley put the car into Drive and slowly pulled away from the curb. He stopped at a parking barrier, fed a machine with more one-dollar bills, then joined a brightly lit highway leading away from the airport.

"Please pro-ceed onto . . . *World Way*," said the GPS.

"So far, so good." Knightley signaled and changed lanes, finding himself surrounded on all sides by large American cars.

"Please turn left onto . . . *Air-port Bou-le-vard*," said the GPS.

"The street names are very helpful," commented Darkus.

The Dodge negotiated the turn, and Darkus stared out the window at the orange sky and the neon facades of the airport hotels. Up ahead were giant billboards for upcoming blockbusters and arteries of traffic extending outward in a sea of headlights and taillights. He thought to himself that Los Angeles really was just how it appeared in the movies.

Tilly loosened her seat belt, switched on the radio, put her feet on the dashboard, and powered down her window to enjoy the warm breeze. Knightley rolled his window down too, draping one hand over the steering wheel and the other over the side of the door. West Coast hip-hop pumped out of the stereo, and the two of them nodded their heads in time.

Then, without warning, both windows rose upward, breaking the moment. Knightley and Tilly whipped their elbows in as the windows slid shut and the radio clicked off.

"What did you press?" Knightley accused her.

"Nothing!" she snapped.

Darkus started pressing the rear window switches. "Dad, have you activated the child locks?"

"I don't *think* I have," Knightley responded.

A warning tone pinged, accompanied by a cluster of red lights on the dashboard.

"Something's wrong with the car," moaned Tilly.

Suddenly, the vehicle changed down a gear and lurched forward, speeding up.

"Speed limit's thirty-five," noted Darkus.

"I'm aware of that, Doc." Knightley looked down to see the accelerator pedal lowering all by itself. "I think I might have selected cruise control . . ."

The display on the GPS inexplicably changed to a different, more complex route. All three occupants did a double take.

"That's not the right way," Tilly pointed out.

Knightley tapped the turn signal and moved the steering wheel to pull over—but it wouldn't budge.

"I can't . . . move . . . the wheel," he complained, then

stepped on the brake, but the pedal sank to the floor with no effect.

Darkus felt his catastrophizer thrum to life, its revs climbing in line with the car engine, whose speedometer needle was gaining steadily. "Tilly, fasten your seat belt," he instructed.

The GPS chimed in with its robotic American accent. "Please sit back and *en-joy the ride* . . ."

Knightley wrestled with the steering wheel, then the wheel began turning by itself. "What the—?"

Darkus and Tilly began examining the car to find out what was controlling it.

The GPS continued its stilted announcement: "The Com-bin-ation would like to extend a warm welcome to all three of you. But un-less you find a way to stop this ve-hicle, this is going to be a v-ery short trip."

"Look at the map," Darkus called out, pointing through the front seats to the display. "It's heading for the ocean."

The GPS continued its speech. "Your move, Knight-leys."

Tilly stabbed the ignition button, but it was useless. "Something must be overriding the engine management system."

"Great. So what do we do about it?" barked Knightley.

The Dodge accelerated around a corner, throwing its occupants and their luggage from one side of the cabin to the other.

"Have a safe jour-ney . . . ," the GPS concluded.

"Try the hand brake!" shouted Darkus.

"I can't find it," replied his dad. "And, for your information, it's called a parking brake in this country."

"There!" Tilly pointed to a small pedal at Knightley's feet.

Knightley stepped on it, but nothing happened. Then he pressed every button on the key fob, but the car continued to gain speed. Knightley tossed the key fob over his shoulder in frustration.

Darkus watched their progress on the map display. "It says arrival time: three minutes." He glanced out at the scenery and got a sinking feeling, seeing an expanse of marshes and bluffs, and off in the distance . . . the Pacific Ocean. Darkus desperately ran his fingers over his chin, trying to deduce a solution, searching for any new hair to twiddle with; then it hit him: "The shaver . . . I need the shaver."

"He's right," yelled Tilly jubilantly. "Thank the lord for Miss Khan. If we can send an electromagnetic pulse, we'll fry the circuitry, shut down the whole vehicle. Where is it?"

"In the boot," said Darkus guiltily. "Well, in this country it's known as the trunk."

"Well, that's just fan-tastic!" screamed Tilly—sounding for a moment just like her father, Clive. She jabbed a finger at the GPS. "Why don't we just ask the nice man to stop the car while you hop out and get it?"

The Dodge careened off a highway exit ramp and down a restricted access road, leaving a cloud of dust in its wake.

"Wait—there is another option," suggested Darkus, rummaging in the backseat.

"What are you doing?" Tilly shrieked impatiently.

Darkus located a lever and yanked it down, causing one of the back seats to fold forward, revealing a space leading to the trunk. The car took another hard turn, hurling him against the door, but then he managed to grab onto a seat belt and crawl through the gap in the seats.

"What are you playing at back there?" bellowed Knightley.

"I just need to get to my bag . . ." Darkus extended his hand through the gap. His fingers located his luggage and groped for the zipper, easing it down to allow entry into the bag.

"Sixty seconds!" Tilly shouted, staring at the GPS display, which showed the cursor rapidly approaching a large blue shape. They were heading straight for the water.

"I can see an abandoned pier of some kind!" said Knightley, seeing the marshland give way to the ocean fast approaching ahead of them.

Darkus desperately pulled out clothes, toiletries, then felt the plastic grip of the shaver. The car swerved, sending it rolling out of his hands across the floor of the trunk. He groped again, finally locating it and shuffling back through the gap as quickly as he could.

"We're out of time!" cried Tilly.

The Dodge barreled through a parking barrier, sending it exploding off its hinges, and sped toward a narrow wooden jetty extending over the water.

Darkus held up the shaver. "I've got it!" He switched it on. It made a routine buzzing noise. He slid out the beard trimmer. Still nothing.

"You really haven't used one of those before, have you!" Tilly scolded him.

"*You have arrived at your dest-ination,*" said the GPS.

"Brace!" shouted Knightley, seeing them running out of road, with the dark blue ocean now visible on all sides.

Darkus pushed the switch in the opposite direction, and suddenly the buzzing stopped, the entire dashboard went dark, the headlights flicked off. But the car kept rolling forward under its own momentum.

Darkus's mind went into overdrive. "The electrics are gone, and so is the electronic braking system. However, the hydraulics are still working." He examined a diagram in his head from physics class. "Dad, pump the brake pedal to increase the brake fluid pressure in the master cylinder!"

"I'm pumping!" hollered Knightley.

The hydraulics engaged, and the car suddenly braked, the tires rapidly decelerating on the splintered wooden boards of the disused pier. Knightley gripped the wheel, his knuckles turning white, and stamped repeatedly on the pedal as the car slid to a halt, only inches from the edge.

"Now engage the parking brake," instructed Darkus calmly.

Knightley engaged the smaller pedal at his feet and let out a sigh of relief. "Well, that was a . . . *close shave?*" He waited for a reaction, only to find his two passengers had already exited the vehicle. He frowned and aped an American accent: "You're welcome."

CHAPTER 9
CHECKING IN

A yellow Toyota Prius taxi pulled up in front of the Renaissance-style stone facade of the Beverly Wilshire Hotel, in the heart of Beverly Hills. The Knightleys and Tilly were squeezed in the backseat, and the trunk lid was tied half open to accommodate their luggage.

A valet jogged to the cab, then signaled two more bell-hops to unload the bags. The Knightleys got out and surveyed the wide boulevard and the rows of curved awnings containing pricey boutiques, all fanned by gently swaying palm trees. Again, Darkus felt like he was in a Hollywood movie—or, in their case, a sinister plot hatched by the Combination.

"Are you sure we can afford this?" he whispered to his dad, staring up at the hotel.

Knightley smiled, taking in the splendor of their surroundings. "Clearly our enemy knew we were coming to America. Uncle Bill never arranged a rental car—it was all a setup. All part of the devious game we're currently engaged in. So, since our existing travel plans have been compromised, it's time to change the rules . . . do something unpredictable."

"Even if it means facing bankruptcy when we return home?" asked Darkus.

"Look at it this way," said his dad. "We could be dead."

"I suppose."

Knightley paused, as if searching for more avenues to justify himself. "No one would expect us to be staying at one of the top hotels in town. It's the perfect cover."

"Sounds good to me," Tilly chimed in, passing her handbag to another bellhop, then sashaying into the marble lobby.

Inside, the trio approached the young woman at the reception desk.

"The name's Alan Knightley. I stayed here a while ago, with the president's security detail."

"Oh, I see," replied the receptionist, impressed.

"In the role of a consultant," Knightley added. "It was the Case of the Star-Spangled Banner, one of my trickiest investigations yet, but one that brought about a very satisfactory result. At least the president thought so."

"Wow, okay."

Darkus delved into his mental case files, but had no memory of the Case of the Star-Spangled Banner. Perhaps his father had no memory of it either.

"So my kids and I are passing through town, and we've had a slight mishap with our rental car and accommodation, so I wondered if you had any rooms available." Before she had a chance to answer, he went on, "Obviously if you were able to arrange an upgrade, I could put in a good word with POTUS himself."

Darkus whispered to Tilly, "That's the Secret Service abbreviation for the president of the United States."

"Yes, I know that. But does he actually *know* him?" asked Tilly quietly.

"I have no evidence that he knows the president, no," muttered Darkus.

"You understand, due to the nature of my job," Knightley continued, "our stay will have to remain absolutely top secret. This conversation never happened."

"Of course, Mr. Knightley . . . ," replied the receptionist, obediently checking her computer screen. "Let me see what I can do."

The bellhop opened the door and wheeled the luggage in on a polished brass cart.

"Welcome to the presidential suite of the Beverly Wilshire," he began. "You have views in three directions, a living room, library, and formal dining room; his and hers walk-in closets, a fifty-five-inch plasma TV, motorized drapery, a state-of-the-art toilet with seat warmer, and a climate-controlled shower. If the suite looks familiar to you, it's because it was made famous in the movie *Pretty Woman*."

"I love that movie," said Tilly.

"Me too," replied Knightley.

The trio looked around in total awe. The bellhop led them past a row of Roman columns, mirrors, and floor-to-ceiling windows, then unloaded their bags onto oak luggage racks.

"Is there anything else I can assist you with?" asked the bellhop, loitering by the door.

Darkus knew the routine, held out his hand to his father, who deposited a wad of one-dollar bills in it, then Darkus passed them to the bellhop.

"Oh, yeah," Tilly piped up. "Where's the hot tub?"

After indulging in a lavish and stratospherically expensive room service delivery of burgers, fries, and chocolate malt shakes—topped off with a sizable tip for the waiter—the Knightleys and Tilly settled down in their separate bedrooms, feeling the effects of changing time zones, a near-death experience, and the troubling nature of their visit.

As Darkus buttoned up the Beverly Wilshire monogrammed pajamas that he'd discovered in the closet (his father was already in the other twin bed wearing his own), he weighed the facts in his mind. Uncle Bill had e-mailed with fresh security camera footage showing Bogna exiting Los Angeles International Airport with Sturgess, before both entered a yellow LA cab that quickly vanished among

a sea of other yellow cabs. In all probability, their house-keeper was still within the city limits, and they had to find her before some harm came to her.

"I thought I told you to trust me," said his father, as if reading his mind.

"I fear we're getting distracted."

"Are you referring to Tilly? She's become a dependable member of the team."

"Proven beyond doubt," Darkus agreed.

"Then you're referring to the case," deduced his father.

Darkus nodded. "We survived the Combination's attempt on our lives today . . . but we can't outwit them forever."

"But if we can buy enough time to find Bogna . . . turn the game in our favor . . . this could be our chance to crack the Combination for good."

Darkus sighed. "It's like looking for a needle in a haystack."

"But Bogna is a particularly unique and peculiar needle, my dear Doc. Now get some rest. Today was a long day, and I fear tomorrow will be even longer."

"I've been thinking . . . ," Darkus said after a brief pause.

"About?" his father inquired blearily.

"This is going to be our last case, Dad." He paused, only half aware of the shock wave he'd just sent through his father. "I'll do my best to find Bogna and bring her home safely. That's a given. But, like you said when we first started working together, this isn't the life for me. It's not what you intended for me, and I don't think it's what I want anymore

either. I think I could be happy with an ordinary profession. A lawyer perhaps. Or a dentist."

Knightley Senior swallowed and went quiet. "I understand, Doc." He searched for the words. "Due to my shortcomings, you have become a target of forces beyond my control. Forces of darkness that have no place in your young world."

Darkus felt a chill and pulled the covers closer around his throat.

"I've always done everything I can to guard you from them," his father went on, "and I will continue to do so. Just know that I won't let you down. Whatever you decide to do with your life, I'll make sure you're safe."

"But how can you possibly do that?" asked Darkus.

"Just trust me," said his father, then lay silently, wrestling with his thoughts for a moment, before adding: "There is one more thing you should know though . . ." Knightley rolled over to face his son in the opposite bed, but found he'd already fallen asleep.

Knightley watched his son for a full minute, debating whether to tell him, then rolled over and went to sleep as well.

CHAPTER 10

A VERY HOLLYWOOD DEATH

Sometimes clues have to be searched for long and hard, turning over every rock and checking every cranny. Other times, the clues simply come to you.

Such was the case when the Knightleys woke from a long slumber and ordered two exotic egg dishes from room service—one served "over easy" and the other a traditional Mexican *huevos rancheros*—along with fresh juices, English Breakfast tea, three kinds of toast, and a pastry basket. The smell of breakfast was so alluring, it even forced Tilly to surface from the opposite bedroom, shielding her eyes from the bright, featureless blue sky outside the window. Bizarrely, Darkus noticed she had managed to find time to change her hair color from jet black to California blond overnight. Darkus directed his attention to the giant plasma TV on the wall to catch up on the morning's news and current affairs, finding a live broadcast in progress.

A female news anchor stared seriously out of one corner

107

of the screen with perfect hair and impossibly smooth, tanned skin. "Over to Chuck, who's live at the scene . . ."

In the main frame, a reporter in a polo shirt stood on a dusty track surrounded by scrub, speaking into a microphone. "Thanks, Camden. We're here at the world-famous Hollywood sign, located in the Hollywood Hills." The TV camera zoomed out to reveal the massive sign propped on the hillside behind the reporter. "It's one of the most recognizable landmarks on the planet. And, as any Los Angeles resident will know, you can't just walk up to the Hollywood sign. Sure, you can hike past it or fly past it, but it's fenced in so you can't get too close. You can look, but you can't touch. But tragically, that didn't deter struggling actor Humphrey Sturgess, a native of Great Britain, who was found dead at the base of the sign early this morning."

"Looks like we've located our suspect," announced Darkus.

"But where's Bogna?" Knightley murmured.

Tilly rubbed her eyes and sat on the sofa next to them, tearing into a Danish.

"That's right, Camden," the reporter carried on. "Mr. Sturgess arrived in the US only two days ago, with stars in his eyes, but now his star has fallen. Fallen forty-five feet, to be exact. A once promising career cruelly snuffed out. Local police are speculating that Mr. Sturgess scaled the high fence surrounding the sign and somehow climbed to the top of the letter *H*, where he was subsequently found in the scrubland below with—we're hearing—a broken neck. Did he jump, or was it an accident? That's something we just don't know."

"Or was he pushed?" speculated Darkus.

The reporter continued: "What we do know is that Sturgess checked into the Sunset Six Motel on Sunset Boulevard two nights ago, in the company of a woman described as somewhere between forty-five and sixty-five years old, approximately five feet tall, heavily built, a hundred and eighty pounds, with a thick European accent. The LAPD is urgently seeking this female travel companion, and anyone with information is advised to call this one-eight-hundred number."

"Great. So now she's a suspect in a murder investigation," said Tilly in between mouthfuls.

"On the contrary," argued Darkus, "our chances of finding Bogna just exponentially increased. The Los Angeles Police Department can begin the painstaking work of locating her in a city of nearly four million people, hopefully narrowing down the avenues of inquiry . . . while we try a different angle of approach." His father and Tilly waited, hanging on his every word. "If we can get to the bottom of who murdered Humphrey Sturgess—for there's no doubt in my mind that he was murdered—then we'll find the person, or people, holding our missing friend." Darkus slid his knife and fork next to each other on the plate and stood up. "I suggest we pay a visit to the Sunset Six Motel at once."

In keeping with Knightley Senior's newfound vacation spirit, the Beverly Wilshire Hotel arranged an even bigger "full-size" rental car, which transported the trio through the grid system of Los Angeles streets with wallowing ease. This time, they chose *not* to use the GPS.

Knightley drove the sedan through Hollywood, past the historic Chinese Theatre and the stars on the sidewalk of the Walk of Fame, before looping down to Sunset Boulevard and the motel in question.

It was a run-down pink building with peeling paint and a *Welcome* sign hanging at an obscene angle from a gateway over the parking lot.

Knightley concluded his tour guide commentary as they pulled into the lot. "In another triumph of American convenience over the Queen's English, 'motel' is quite simply a hotel where you can park outside your room. A combination of hotel and motor. 'Mo-tel.'"

Darkus ignored him and instructed Tilly. "You create a distraction. I'll process the scene."

"What about me?" his father asked.

"Just stay here and try to look natural," suggested Tilly. "Not easy for you, I know; just watch and learn." She put on a pair of star-shaped sunglasses and got out.

"But—" Knightley began.

"Remember, Dad," said Darkus, "no one suspects a kid."

Darkus got out and approached the drab motel complex, discovering yellow police tape cordoning off one of the second-floor rooms and a pair of LAPD officers sitting on the hood of a patrol car eating doughnuts. Meanwhile, Tilly sauntered toward the swimming pool in a fenced area on the other side of the parking lot. Finding the gate locked, she quickly scaled it and flipped backward onto the other side.

A few moments later, a plop and a light splash emanated from the pool.

"Officer? Excuse me, officers?" Tilly called out from the water, still wearing her star-shaped sunglasses. "I seem to have fallen into the pool. And look, some dipstick left the life preserver out of reach," she spluttered, pointing to the rubber ring floating aimlessly several yards away. It was clear to Darkus that Tilly was responsible for this unfortunate chain of events.

The officers looked at each other, irritated.

Tilly ducked her head under the water, feigning drowning, then spat, "Help! Somebody!"

The officers stuffed the remains of their doughnuts into their mouths and began clambering over the fence into the pool area.

Meanwhile, Darkus quietly ducked under the police tape and climbed the stairway to the second floor. He sneaked under a second length of tape and knelt by the seedy motel room door, taking out a laminated library card that he kept on him for just such occasions. The splashing increased as Tilly was dramatically hauled from the pool, giving Darkus time to slide the card between the lock and the doorjamb, bending the card back and forth a few times. It was an old trick but an effective one, especially on old mechanisms. The latch bolt obediently retracted to grant him entry.

Darkus crept across the dark brown carpet past a pair of twin beds, knowing he had a matter of minutes to conduct his search. He scanned the room's contents, deducing that the accommodation was cheap, rarely cleaned, and used by both the morally and financially bankrupt. This was certainly not the Hollywood dream Sturgess had been promised. His luggage was open and his clothes were strewn across one of the beds: floral-print Hawaiian shirts, harem pants, flip-flops, a pair of Speedo swimming trunks. Evidently his bags had already been searched by the local police. Darkus noted a small jar of styling wax, no doubt for the actor's signature walrus mustache—*May it rest in peace*, he thought. The other bed was still made, and there was no sign of any of Bogna's belongings. He checked the bathroom and found one lone toothbrush, and only one set of used towels. So perhaps Bogna hadn't stayed overnight. In which case, where was she? He returned to the bedroom and glanced under the beds, finding only a collection of "dust bunnies"—a curious and disgusting American term for small balls of lint and fluff. Then he spotted a bottle of prescription pills on a table by the TV. The label had an unpronounceable name that Darkus deduced was a sedative of some kind: no doubt the sleeping pill that Sturgess—or an accomplice—had slipped into the unfortunate housekeeper's drink to guarantee her compliance and easy transportation. Darkus reached for the minibar in a fridge under the TV. He searched it, clearing aside the miniature liquor bottles to reveal . . . a large jar of Polish dill pickles, which was half full. This was the concrete evidence he required. No one except Bogna could consume pickles in that quantity with only limited time. No one. This was proof positive that Bogna had been there, at least for long enough to have a snack; then she was presumably taken elsewhere before night fell. The unfortunate Sturgess had no idea his job had by that point been completed, and his destiny was to be another out-of-work actor—this time *permanently*.

Darkus raised the slats of the blinds to see the two cops kneeling by Tilly, who was gamely pretending to be unconscious on the poolside, intermittently spouting water from her mouth.

Darkus had a last look around, then noticed a collection of bound letter-sized pages among the strewn garments. He picked it up and examined the title page. It read:

AREA 51
A screenplay by
Chuck Penn

Darkus knew enough about the film industry to know that a screenplay was the blueprint for a movie: the action, the scenes, the dialogue—everything was written down for the crew to carry out their work and the actors to learn their lines before the cameras started rolling. Near the bottom of the title page was a recent date stamp and the words:

CLORR ENTERTAINMENT

9601 WILSHIRE BOULEVARD, SUITE #1301
BEVERLY HILLS, CA 90210

Darkus took one more glance through the blinds and saw one of the cops attempting CPR to "save" Tilly's life. Darkus knew the game would soon be up, and took the screenplay, bundled it into the armpit of his safari-style jacket, retraced his steps, and exited the room.

Tilly spied Darkus out of the corner of a half-closed eye, then managed to spray water directly into the cop's face before wiping her mouth in disgust, opening her eyes, and leaning up to chastise him. "What are you doing, huh? I'm absolutely fine. Never felt better."

The cops watched, bewildered, as Tilly got to her feet, collected her purse, gracefully scaled the fence, flipped down onto the other side, and hopped into the rental car. Darkus was already sitting in the backseat.

"Any questions?" she asked Knightley Senior, who obediently put the car in reverse and backed away.

Twenty minutes later, the trio pulled up outside the glass-fronted office building on the corner of 9601 Wilshire Boulevard: the address on the title page of the screenplay—or "script," as it was commonly known. Knightley managed to park the full-size rental car in one of the even bigger parking spots, then followed his young colleagues into the foyer.

A large sign over the reception desk listed the names of all the companies in the building.

"We're here for the audition," Tilly began. "With Clorr Entertainment."

Knightley Senior loitered in the background, not wishing to cramp their style.

"Well, I don't have a record of a casting call today. What are your names?" The male receptionist looked from Tilly to Darkus and back again.

"The Knightleys," Darkus chimed in, presenting his ID. "With an *E-Y*. We're from England."

"*Knightley* . . ." The receptionist's eyes lit up. "Are you related to Keir—?"

"We're her cousins," said Darkus. "Once removed."

"Well, Clorr Entertainment is on the fifth floor. Go on up, and good luck!"

Knightley Senior followed along behind. "I'm with them."

They took the elevator to the fifth floor and stepped out to find a slick, dimly lit corridor lined with offices and hung with framed posters of recent blockbuster movies. An assistant brushed past them without a second glance. Darkus led the way past several glass doorways until they reached a solid door with an eye-catching logo showing a C inside a circle. Beside it were the words *Clorr Entertainment*. He tried the handle and found it unlocked. He teased it open.

Inside, the office was completely empty. A reception desk appeared abandoned. The phone was unplugged. There were no posters on the walls, no computers or filing cabinets, just a handful of wheelie chairs scattered across a derelict boardroom. It was as if the office had never been used.

"It's a front company of some kind," remarked Darkus. "It's not real."

"What about the script?" asked Tilly. "That's real. Someone must have written it."

"Dad, has Bill run the name yet?"

Knightley glanced at his phone screen and nodded grimly. "Chuck Penn—perhaps unsurprisingly—is a pseudonym. A pen name. A fake. He's not represented by any of the major agencies, and there's no address on file at the Writers Guild. Like the company he works for, Clorr Entertainment, he doesn't seem to exist."

"Is everything in LA fake?" pondered Tilly.

"It would appear so," Darkus responded.

"Not everything," countered his father, staring into the

middle distance. "I once solved a case here . . . the Mystery of the Fallen Angeleno."

Darkus explained to Tilly, "Angeleno is a term for a native Los Angeles resident . . . oh, wait a second." Darkus performed his own thousand-yard stare, consulting his father's case files in his head. "I must be getting rusty myself. You solved that case with the help of a pair of local Angelenos: a pair of LA private detectives, if I'm not mistaken."

"You're right, Doc, I did!"

Tilly observed the two of them as if they were conjoined aliens, sharing one brain.

"If my memory serves me correctly," Darkus went on, digging deeper into the Knowledge, "their phone number was 323-555-1200."

Tilly shook her head, half impressed, half spooked.

"Excellent, Doc!" said Knightley, beaming with pride, then checking his watch. "I'll invite them to brunch."

"Brunch?" said Darkus.

"Surely you know what that means," demanded Tilly. "It's a cross between breakfast and lunch."

Darkus nodded. "Yes, but we only just had breakfast."

"Correct again," replied Knightley, "but over here, no one's counting."

CHAPTER 11
BRADLEY & SON

Contact was made, and the agreed rendezvous point was a diner called Swingers. The trio were seated by a long window lined with plaid-patterned leatherette booths, Formica tables, and waitresses in T-shirts, skirts, and knee-high boots. Knightley watched the door while Darkus and Tilly ordered two large, thick malt shakes to begin with, before struggling with an even larger menu than they'd previously witnessed. They each unfolded their copy as if reading the Sunday papers and sucked on the shakes until their faces ached.

At precisely noon the glass doors swung open, and Knightley stood up to greet his LA partners in crime-solving. This time it was Darkus and Tilly's turn to do a double take: the local investigators were a father and son, both dressed in matching green plaid, three-piece suits—fashioned out of a more lightweight cotton than the Knightleys' customary tweed, Darkus observed. The duo were African American, approximately the same height and build as Darkus and his dad, and possessed the same acute gaze that betrayed the minds of great detectives.

Darkus stood up to join his father, out of respect and amazement, greeting their near mirror image standing before them.

"Doc, meet Irwin and Rufus Bradley. Also known as . . . Bradley & Son. Los Angeles's finest private investigators."

Darkus extended his hand.

"Rufus," the younger Bradley introduced himself, shaking Darkus's hand, then making a fist. Darkus got the meaning, also made a fist, and they bumped them together.

"Bring it in, Alan." Bradley Senior embraced Knightley Senior fondly.

"It's been a long time, Irwin," he replied. "Meet our newest addition to the team. This is Tilly."

She stood up and shook Irwin's hand before exchanging a complex handshake with Rufus that involved a fist bump, a snap, and a flurry of fingers ending in an explosion.

Rufus nodded, impressed. "Where did you learn that?"

"The Web," Tilly responded.

"Please," said Knightley, gesturing to the booth. "Order yourselves something, and let's begin the briefing."

"I should warn you. I gave up meat, wheat, caffeine, and dairy," said Irwin. "Doctor's orders."

"Me too," added Rufus.

"Very wise, I'm sure," Knightley admitted. "But for myself, life's too short. Now to business . . ."

Bradley & Son listened intently as Knightley brought them up to speed on the investigation so far. When the Bradleys occasionally interrupted the flow with their own observations and deductions, Darkus had the uncanny impression of watching himself and his father talking, so similar were the Bradleys' demeanors and intellects. Darkus and Tilly chimed in with any details Knightley had overlooked; but nobody mentioned the puzzle box or the hard drive, out of respect for Tilly's private mission to destroy all those responsible for her mother's death—the details of which were still being decoded by her hacker colleagues online.

As the briefing drew to a close, Bradley Senior turned to his son. "Well, Rufus, what do you make of this?"

"Undoubtedly a trap of some kind," the boy began. "With Miss Bogna as bait. But then why would the Combination go to the trouble of playing games and trying to bump them off on arrival? Do the bad guys want them to find Bogna or not? Beats me, because it appears your housekeeper is of no inherent value to the enemy."

"Not that I can think of," replied Knightley.

"But she is of great sentimental value to all three of us," noted Darkus.

"So is she just a pawn in the game?" Rufus speculated. "And if so . . . what is the game?"

"Precisely," said Darkus.

"Alan, I think you'll agree that this calls for a reasoned approach," advised Irwin. "We begin with the facts, then arrange them into a number of possible theories until the most probable one appears."

Knightley nodded. "The only facts we have so far are that Bogna is missing, and Clorr Entertainment promised her now deceased kidnapper a role in a movie called *Area 51*."

"You all know what Area 51 is, right?" Rufus addressed the group.

"Only a little bit," replied Darkus modestly, before elaborating. "It's a top-secret US Air Force base in the Nevada desert about four hundred miles from here. It was formally known as Groom Lake, originally founded in the 1940s as a reserve airfield before later becoming a testing ground for experimental aircraft and cutting-edge military technology."

"A-plus," said Irwin. "And it's also rumored to be where UFOs are taken when they crash-land, so the US government can harvest them for research. The ships, that is. Hell, maybe the aliens too."

"Hold up, Pops," Rufus interjected. "There's no concrete evidence of any actual alien life reaching planet earth. Let's stay in the realm of reality, shall we?"

"Once again, I agree," said Darkus.

Irwin glanced at Knightley Senior and shrugged. "Kids, eh?"

"When will they learn?" sighed Knightley.

"Oh, you know they will," chuckled Irwin.

Rufus continued undaunted. "Other nicknames for Area 51 include Dreamland and Paradise Ranch. The facility is classified *above* top secret. The airspace and a six-hundred-square-mile area around it are totally restricted. Obviously it's ripe for use in fiction, which is probably why your mysterious screenwriter, Chuck Penn, decided to write a movie about it."

"Sounds like the perfect base for the Combination," said Tilly, licking her lips, either from the malt shake or the anticipated taste of vengeance.

Darkus noticed her brooding demeanor and tried to keep the investigation on track. "Right now, that script is the only evidence we've got," he reminded them. "I started reading it on the way over here, and I must confess it's extremely poorly executed. It concerns a group of campers and an escaped alien. The action is unrealistic, the plot is preposterous, and the characterization is all over the place."

"Well, fortunately for you, Rufus and I are well connected within the industry, and I predict we can deliver you this 'Chuck Penn' in a matter of hours," said Irwin.

A waitress arrived with their orders. "Okay, who had the tofu scramble with lettuce instead of toast?"

"That would be me," Irwin confessed.

"And the double bacon cheeseburger with chili fries and everything on it?" inquired the waitress.

Knightley meekly raised a hand. "When in Rome."

CHAPTER 12
THE BIG BREAK

After a few well-placed phone calls, the Bradleys informed the Knightleys that Chuck Penn was a new writer on the scene, having previously worked in a now defunct DVD store in a place called Van Nuys in the San Fernando Valley. Penn's real name was Melvin Neumann, and he resided with his parents in a bungalow in a cul-de-sac by the noisy 101 freeway, a ten-lane superhighway that linked Los Angeles in the south with San Francisco in the north and appeared to be congested with cars and big-rig trucks at all times of day and night.

Bradley & Son drove their esteemed visitors to the Neumanns' address in the back of their souped-up yellow Los Angeles cab—a Ford Crown Victoria, designed to blend in as effortlessly as Knightley's Fairway cab did back home. On arrival, Bradley Senior and Knightley Senior made the first approach.

After ringing twice, the door opened to reveal a

middle-aged lady in a velour tracksuit with rhinestones embroidered on it. "Can I help you?" she asked.

"Mrs. Neumann?" Irwin held up his private investigator's license. "We'd like to interview your son, Melvin."

"Well, what's he done?" she demanded. "Tell me he hasn't bought something he can't afford. Melvin??!" she hollered into the entrance hall behind her. "There are two men in suits to see you."

In the background, Knightley detected feet running across a carpet, followed by a window being raised in haste. "Madam, would you mind if we came in?" he suggested.

"Well, with an accent like that, you can stay for tea!"

Knightley smiled and stepped past her, rapidly following the noises down a short corridor to a closed bedroom door. As Knightley opened the door, he saw a leg vanish through the sash window and drop to the AstroTurf below.

"We've got a runner," he shouted back to Bradley.

In the yellow cab outside, Darkus saw a short man in his mid-twenties stumble away from the bungalow and attempt a sprint across the backyard before hurling himself over the neighbor's fence.

Darkus, Rufus, and Tilly leaped out of the cab and gave chase. Neumann, while not naturally athletic or coordinated, was unusually talented at evasive action. He dodged around the neighbor's inflatable swimming pool, hopped onto a trampoline, and ricocheted over the next neighbor's fence. Tilly followed suit, hurdling the trellis while Darkus and Rufus tracked the runner's progress from the row of tidy front yards lining the cul-de-sac. Before long, Knightley Senior and Bradley Senior were jogging after their junior colleagues, panting and breaking a sweat.

Neumann reached the end of the row of backyards and vanished into a bush at the base of a steep incline, leading straight upward to the loudly buzzing 101 freeway. A moment later the writer appeared halfway up the slope, frantically climbing toward the guardrail, which was only yards from the torrent of vehicles flashing past.

"Stop!" shouted Rufus. "We only want to talk!"

"I haven't done anything wrong!" yelled Neumann.

"No one said you did!" Darkus called out.

Tilly arrived at the base of the incline and joined the appeal. "What are you running for?"

Neumann gulped for breath following his exertions, then flopped himself over the guardrail, half fell onto the other side, and staggered toward the traffic, contemplating a hopeless escape route.

"Stop!" shrieked Tilly as all three of them raced up the hill.

They found Neumann frozen in fear at the sight of five lines of cars and trucks zipping by at a dozen per second. Beyond the central divider there were another five lanes of fast-moving traffic traveling in the opposite direction.

Darkus made a brief calculation, then called over to

Neumann from the emergency lane. "I estimate your chances of survival to be less than one in a thousand."

Rufus nodded. "I concur."

"Melvin!" shouted Tilly. "I loved your script," she lied. "You're a brilliant writer."

Neumann turned, his face breaking into a snaggle-toothed smile. "Really? You think so?"

"You bet. Come back over here and I'll tell you everything I loved about it," she went on, admittedly feeling a little bad about the deception.

Darkus and Rufus watched in amazement as Tilly talked him back from the edge.

Mrs. Neumann made coffee while her son, Melvin, wept in the front room.

"So you didn't read it at all?" he sobbed.

"Well, I loved the title," said Tilly, on the sofa next to him. "Short and punchy. Just like you."

Rufus took over the interview. "Melvin . . . why did you skip out on us? What are you so afraid of?"

Neumann blew his nose loudly, then squeezed the handkerchief back into the front pocket of his chinos. "This was my big break. The producers told me the script had a green light, casting was under way, and the movie was going into production next month."

"Well, technically, casting *had* started . . . ," said Darkus, before realizing he probably shouldn't disclose the fate of the intended star, Humphrey Sturgess. "But one of the actors, well . . . dropped out."

"What are the names of the producers?" asked Knightley. "Can you give us a description?"

"No. It was all done by e-mail. They never used names, only initials, and they were different initials each time. Two days ago I got a message saying they'd pulled the plug. The money fell through."

"That must have been a hard knock," Tilly consoled him.

"But that wasn't the worst part," Neumann confessed. "They said their backers weren't happy, and they weren't the sort of people to mess with. They said I couldn't breathe a word about the script. They threatened me with legal action—or worse. So when two dudes in suits showed up . . . ," he said, gesturing to Knightley Senior and Bradley Senior, "well, I assumed the worst."

"What were the producers so hung up about?" asked Irwin.

"They told me they owned the rights to the story, and I had to keep my mouth shut about it. Especially about Yucca Flat."

Darkus's ears pricked up. "Yucca Flat?"

Rufus explained to his British colleague privately: "Yucca Flat is a former nuclear testing range in the Nevada desert. A total no-go zone. Over eight hundred nuclear tests took place there between the years 1951 and 1991. It sits directly next to Area 51."

Darkus felt his catastrophizer hum to life, ticking persistently, telling him that something was afoot. "So the movie you wrote was going to be filmed there, in Yucca Flat?" he inquired.

Neumann nodded. "That's where they wanted it. They wanted somewhere remote and cut-off. Impossible to find. They asked me to do some research on the ghost towns out there. The ones with all the mannequins in them. The ones they used to use to simulate nuclear explosions."

Darkus had seen the images before: houses being turned inside out and swept away by an unnatural man-made power; windows shattering and paint being scorched off; life-sized plastic figures of families sitting around the dinner table before being incinerated by the hot fission blast of an atomic weapon. It was the stuff of worst nightmares.

Neumann went on, "They wanted me to write a scene in one of these towns. Where a hostage is being held prisoner against her will."

Darkus felt his catastrophizer shift up a gear. "Bogna . . ."

Tilly looked at him and nodded in agreement. "Melvin, do you know the exact location where they were going to be filming?"

"Sure, it's called Survival Town. But you won't find anyone living there. Except a few plastic dummies."

"The scene you wrote . . . ," Darkus pressed him, "how did it end?"

"A bomb went off and they were all wiped out," replied Neumann, with tears in his eyes. "It was awesome."

Improbable as it may have sounded, it was perfectly possible for an out-of-work screenwriter to be hired to construct the plotline for a real-life kidnapping. Darkus had heard rumors of a group of Hollywood screenwriters hired by America's Central Intelligence Agency in the aftermath of September 11 for a very similar purpose: to construct possible scenarios for future terrorist attacks, so that these attacks could be prepared for and hopefully thwarted. The writers were told to give their imagination free rein—just as the terrorists had. Melvin Neumann may not be winning any Oscars anytime soon, but he had successfully found a location so far off the map that it perfectly fit the bill for stowing a hostage. Melvin might have missed out on his big break in Hollywood, but Darkus had just gotten his big break in the case. It was only a lead, and not yet a certainty, but he was convinced that Bogna was being held in Survival Town, Nevada.

What better place to hide someone than in a place that wasn't supposed to exist?

CHAPTER 13
THE EXTRATERRESTRIAL HIGHWAY

The Knightleys and the Bradleys agreed to meet in the hotel lobby at 9 p.m., giving both families time to regroup before setting out for the desert by nightfall.

It turned out that Irwin Bradley also had an ex-wife, Angie, whom he had to make excuses to; and, from what Darkus could tell, Angie still loved Irwin, as Darkus suspected his own mother still loved his father. It brought into sharp focus how dearly Darkus wanted his parents to get back together, even though the whole situation felt like a dropped pie that would take an army of people to clean up. Wolseley Close, as long as Clive was in it, was never going to be home. That was part of the reason Darkus chose detective work over the domestic strife he'd had to endure all those years. Though neither of them made reference to it, Darkus sensed that he and Rufus shared the same feelings about their outlandish dads and long-suffering moms. As detectives do, they weighed opposing theories, they understood both sides of the argument, but they still wished for a solution—no matter how unrealistic that dream might be.

Almost as if Jackie knew her son was thinking about her, the secure phone rang and the word *Mum* appeared on the screen. Remembering his dad's strict instructions to keep her out of the investigation for as long as possible—for her own safety—and even though Darkus longed to hear her reassuring voice, he let it ring and ring until it went to voice mail. The secure phone would reroute the call and disguise the ringtone so she wouldn't know that he was currently on the other side of the world. After a few moments, he checked the message.

"Hi, darling, it's your mom here," Jackie's voice said chirpily on the message. Even the ambient noise of the kitchen reminded him of home. "I've got some exciting news to tell you. I know you're busy with your dad, but if you can, give me a call. I'm here for another few hours, then I'm . . . well, I'll tell you when I see you. Love you." She hung up.

Much as Darkus wanted to know what this news was, he decided to trust his dad. With any luck, Bogna would soon be safely back in pocket and they could return to England, and maybe, just maybe, family life would slowly take the shape he dreamed of . . . and the dropped pie could be cleared up.

*

In her own room at the other end of the suite, Tilly stared at her smartphone. The timer had reached twenty-four hours and forty-nine minutes, with the seconds steadily ticking down until the contents of Underwood's hard drive would be revealed. It was probably a daydream to think that the solution to all her problems would just pop up on a screen. And when she finally got the names of everyone responsible for her mother's death, if she tracked them down one by one, would it make her feel any better? Would she be able to shed the enormous burden of loss on her shoulders? Or would it only make things worse? Almost as if the phone knew it was being watched, the handset buzzed, and she checked her e-mail inbox.

Her eyebrows lowered into two acute angles as she opened the message. It read:

T*
First installment attached.
Will send u the rest in 24 hrs.
Peace.
*^M^*

It was Mike, her associate from the dark cloud—she didn't know his last name, and never asked. She moved her finger toward the attachment and felt her hands go red-hot with anticipation, as if the phone were on fire. She tapped on the file, sat down on the edge of the bed, and began to read . . .

133

An hour later, the Knightleys and Tilly crossed the lobby carrying their backpacks and kitbags. Knightley informed the receptionist that they were going on an impromptu camping trip, and, not wishing to question a close associate of the president, she smiled and waved.

The Bradleys waited outside in a blacked-out Chevy Suburban SUV, complete with off-road tires, roof-mounted spotlights, and heavy-duty bull bars and grilles. The route to Survival Town had been mapped out. They had to avoid Area 51 itself at all costs, or risk a mammoth response from whatever military units were active there; not to mention the possibility of aliens, UFOs, and the paranormal, which Knightley continued to remind them of.

Darkus felt he was taking a journey not only into the unknown, but into one of the least known corners of American history.

The Knightleys and Tilly climbed into the large back-seat, with Irwin and Rufus sitting up front. The dashboard was ablaze with flashing lights from radar detectors and police scanners. Knightley nudged Darkus in the ribs, impressed. If anyone could help them find Bogna, Darkus was confident it was the Bradleys. Tilly remained silent as the car quickly left Beverly Hills and took the on-ramp to the nearest freeway, which was never far from reach.

Los Angeles took on an eerie glow in the night. The palm

trees were still painted orange, this time by neon instead of sunshine. The billboards broadcast their images to empty streets and discreet homeless encampments. Office buildings loomed overhead, half lit and completely deserted. Even the freeways were almost devoid of traffic, except for an occasional convoy of big-rig trucks or a sedan with tinted windows disguising the identity and motive of its occupants. Irwin Bradley navigated the city with just the palm of his left hand on the power steering, while the other lay relaxed on the center console.

Outside the Bradleys' own tinted windows, the city receded below them as they climbed the 405 interstate over the hills and down into the San Fernando Valley, where the landscape flattened out into an endless basin of lights. Darkus turned to Tilly, finding her unusually quiet. She either didn't notice him or didn't acknowledge him, and just kept staring into the luminous grid. They followed the superhighway through more ten-lane-wide inclines carved out of the hills, until it became a two-lane blacktop and the desert opened up around them, revealing what an oasis LA had been. Epic stretches of dusty lunar landscape extended on all sides, with only occasional road signs and street lamps to light the way. Darkus glimpsed the odd stainless-steel Airstream camper parked among the rocks and wondered who on earth would choose to live there—and why?

After several hours on the same unending road, punctuated only by isolated motels and gas stations, Darkus and his father nodded off, until Irwin cranked his head around from the driver's seat.

"We're coming up on Route 375, also known as the E.T. Highway. That stands for 'extraterrestrial,' obviously. There have been more UFO sightings reported on this stretch of road than anywhere else in the world."

Darkus rubbed his eyes and looked out into the darkness. The desert was flat and featureless, apart from a range of hills just visible in the distance. The night sky displayed a constellation of stars twinkling from outer space, as if they knew they were being observed. A green road sign announced the Extraterrestrial Highway, the metal spattered with bullet holes, stickers of American flags, and drawings of UFOs.

Irwin pulled the SUV into a lonely gas station and got out to fill the tank.

Tilly stayed in the car while the Knightleys stretched their legs, entering the attached convenience store.

"Nice night, ain't it?" grunted the cashier, a large bearded man in denim overalls and a trucker hat. Talk radio rattled out of an old stereo.

Darkus noticed a row of plastic action figures lined up behind the counter, then realized they were all little green men with reptilian eyes and no ears: *aliens*. With some trepidation, Darkus noticed the cashier's hat had a slogan on it: *They're Out There!*

Knightley smiled, feeling right at home, finding a model

of a flying saucer suspended over the coolers. He selected a bottle of water for Darkus and a Dr Pepper for himself, then approached the cashier.

"Excuse me, sir." Knightley put a couple of dollar bills on the counter. "Have you ever actually *seen* an Unidentified Flying Object?"

The cashier looked up from his magazine. "Seen one?" he squeaked. "How 'bout every darn night? Just over that ridge . . ." He pointed a grubby finger through the window. "Like the Fourth o' July." He let out a hysterical giggle.

"Can you describe what you saw?" Darkus inquired from beside his father.

"On the inside or the outside?" the man responded, adjusting his overalls.

"You've seen the inside?" asked Darkus, confused.

"Oh, sure. When I got abducted by a couple of grays over at Billy Bob's."

"Grays?" asked Darkus.

Knightley gently guided his son away from the counter, explaining privately: "'Grays' is a term for light-skinned aliens. But I fear this witness is not to be relied upon."

The Knightleys got back into the SUV, and Irwin pulled out of the service station with Rufus riding shotgun.

Darkus noticed Tilly still staring into the night, her hand clutching the smartphone, her knuckles showing white. "Is everything okay?" he asked her.

"Never been better," she murmured.

Not wishing to trigger the fine trip wires of her personality, Darkus left her alone in a cocoon of silence. The stress of waiting for answers was taking its toll on Tilly. Or there was something else going on—but Darkus couldn't deduce what.

Just then, Knightley leaped out of his seat and pointed through the window. "*Look! There . . .*"

Incredibly, in the night sky, four brilliant white lights appeared on the horizon, then scorched a path upward in rapid succession, each following their own trajectory.

"I don't believe it," shouted Knightley excitedly, grinning like a child. "*Real* UFOs!"

Darkus followed his father's gaze and saw them too; then he furrowed his brow, not sure what to make of them. They appeared to accelerate and disperse with such smooth, steady velocity. Strangely, the Bradleys didn't even look twice.

"Hate to break it to you, Alan," said Irwin, "but they're military flares, released to guide airplanes into Area 51 under the cover of night."

"Ah," said Knightley, deflated.

"But what type of airplanes they're guiding in," Rufus elaborated, "and why they're flown there at night—that's a whole other mystery. Early prototypes resulted in innovations like the stealth bomber."

"He's right, Dad," said Darkus. "There are even theories

that UFOs were just a smoke screen created by the US government to cover up their own technological advances."

"Next time, I shall be more rigorous in my deductions," Knightley apologized.

Irwin informed his passengers, "Okay, things might get a little rough."

The SUV detoured right off the highway onto a dust track. Tilly and the Knightleys took hold of the overhead handles as the Chevy went off-road, bouncing and lurching over the uneven surface, its knobby tires throwing up rocks and sand in their wake. Outside, Darkus noticed a faded government sign that read:

WARNING. RESTRICTED AREA.

NO TRESPASSING BEYOND THIS POINT.

PHOTOGRAPHY IS PROHIBITED.

Behind it, a high wire fence extended along the crest of the hills.

"Switch to infrared," Irwin instructed his son.

"Ten-four, Pops." Rufus pressed a row of switches that turned off the vehicle's headlights, taillights, and even the dashboard.

Bradley & Son then flipped down their sun visors, which each contained night vision goggles that they quickly strapped to their faces. The SUV skirted the perimeter of the restricted area and entered a vast valley with dunes looming on either side.

"Off to your left you'll see the infamous Groom Lake, aka Area 51," Irwin announced like a tour guide.

In the distance, Darkus could make out a community of white, rectangular aircraft hangars and a set of runways, like a concrete village at the base of a small mountain range. The whole area was fenced off with checkpoints and razor wire. A few floodlights were the only signs of life.

The SUV bounced farther into the desert, crossing an enormous dry lake bed, navigating a wide path around the restricted area, before progressing deeper into the former nuclear testing ground.

"We'll have to hike the last mile or two, to avoid detection," said Irwin as he pulled the SUV over in a cloud of dust.

Darkus and the others got out and shouldered their backpacks. The ground was rocky, dotted with parched, skeletal bushes and teeming with tumbleweeds rolling in the direction of the breeze. The only illumination came from the coin-like edge of a crescent moon.

"Look out for rattlers," advised Rufus.

"Snakes?" said Knightley, alarmed. "Nobody mentioned those."

Irwin led the group into the bleak scrubland in single file.

"That'll be to disguise our numbers," Darkus told Tilly, but was met with a disinterested shrug.

140

They cut across the brow of a hill, then descended through dense brush and cactus trees, reaching a flat plain. In the distance the moonlight picked out gaping, circular craters stretching as far as the eye could see. The chasms were perfectly round, ranging from approximately a hundred to a thousand yards in diameter, and evenly spaced in geometric patterns. Darkus realized these were entirely man-made: the result of decades of underground nuclear testing.

A white metal sign stood straight up in the ruined earth, with a warning:

RADIATION HAZARD. TOUCHING OR REMOVING
SCRAP OBJECTS IS PROHIBITED.

A hundred yards away, they saw an even stranger sight: the chassis of a classic American car, charred and twisted by an unimaginable force. Beside it was a collection of long steel rods, like dropped toothpicks, that had once formed the reinforced concrete of a building. Darkus felt his catastrophizer jittering unevenly at the back of his head like a compass needle jumping at a magnetic field, or a Geiger counter detecting a radioactive charge. The fallout here had long settled or been blown elsewhere by the wind, but the memory remained. More so than all the crime scenes he'd ever witnessed, there was something very wrong about this place.

Tilly was visibly shaken too, though it did nothing to change her mood—in fact, it seemed to match it. Darkus suspected she was bottling up a highly flammable emotion that could go nuclear and tear them apart at any moment. The tension was compounded by the specter of the Combination looming over every step of the investigation. Darkus wondered: had they really outplayed the enemy? Or were they being watched at this very moment?

Darkus continued after the Bradleys as a familiar square shape emerged from the gloom. It was a house: a mock home that had somehow been saved from the annihilation, perhaps fortunate enough to be standing just outside the blast radius. Around it were an array of half-destroyed structures; some with supporting walls still standing, but the roofs blown off; some reduced to blocks with wires protruding like torn ligaments; others simply razed to the ground.

Irwin checked a GPS device and confirmed: "Welcome to Survival Town."

CHAPTER 14
SURVIVAL TOWN

"This is all that's left?" said Darkus, inspecting the single family home.

"It would appear so," replied Irwin.

The mock house was clad in wooden boards, the windows were long shattered and gone, but the frames were still intact. A neatly pointed brick chimney extended upward, but there was no light or life within the building's walls.

It appeared that nobody was home.

Darkus took a small penlight from his top pocket and approached the doorway, which lacked a door. His father quickly stopped his arm and led the way instead. The others watched cautiously.

The Knightleys crept over the front step, and Darkus angled the penlight from behind his father, illuminating the faded decorations of a living room, casting long shadows across the peeling walls. Knightley Senior stepped inside the room while Darkus panned with the flashlight beam, until—

A face leered up at them, its arm reaching out for theirs. Knightley grabbed his son in fright.

"It's okay, Dad. It's just a dummy."

Darkus focused the beam on the figure: a grossly distorted mannequin, still dressed in a business suit, its eyes staring out, its head partly caved in, and its limbs bent in unnatural angles. Darkus swallowed his fear.

Knightley Senior caught his breath. "I believe I'm the dummy."

"Bogna . . . ?" Darkus called out into the dead air of the house.

There was no response.

Darkus continued to probe the room with his penlight, picking out a living room with a sofa, the remains of a TV set, and a kitchen complete with cupboards and a stove. Then he flinched as he saw the rest of the mannequin's family in various poses around a dining table. The wife was wearing an apron, her shoulders hunched over and her head planted facedown on a dinner plate. Two children, one with short hair, one with pigtails, had fallen off their chairs and were lying in abject positions surrounded by cutlery. Darkus started as a large rodent scampered across the kitchen counter, rattling the china and vanishing behind a cupboard door.

Feeling a shudder, Darkus crept over the terrifying human figures and followed the flashlight beam through a narrow hallway to a back room.

"Bogna?!" Knightley yelled.

"Dad . . ." Darkus beckoned him down the hallway.

The floorboards were covered in a fine layer of dust and desert sand, revealing several footprints circling the room.

Darkus knelt down and observed three sets of distinct prints. "Size twelve Crocs," he noted, pointing at one set with a sharpened pencil that he'd plucked from his top pocket.

"Bogna," his father confirmed with a nod. "Once again, we're too late. Judging by the size and inflection of the other prints, she had two heavyset captors. They'd need to be to contain her."

On a dressing table, Darkus spotted a familiar straw hat. "It's the one she wore at Heathrow."

"But where is she now . . . ?" replied his father anxiously. "If she tried to make a break for it, she could die out there."

Darkus found it difficult to grasp the concept of Bogna dying of hunger, thirst, or exposure. She had the constitution of an ox, the determination of a pit bull, and the strength of several men.

Instead, he turned his mind to the here and now and followed the concentration of male footprints to a rickety side table with a small, blank notepad sitting on it. He flipped through the pages, hunting for clues but finding only blank sheets. He took his pencil and scribbled on the top page, shading it to see if any indentations might betray themselves. The shading produced no meaningful inscriptions: no words; just a doodle depicting a simple triangle. Darkus kept scribbling, revealing a two-dimensional pyramid shape.

"Does this mean anything to you?" he asked his father.

"Not really," Knightley replied, looking over his shoulder. "I suppose it could refer to the conspiracy theory surrounding the Egyptian pyramids."

"Huh?"

"The Egyptian pyramids exactly match a pyramid rumored to have been found on the dark side of the moon by the last manned lunar landing, Apollo 17, in 1972. Presumably it was the work of an alien civilization."

"O–kay, Dad," said Darkus dismissively.

"Don't you think it odd that we've never been back to the moon since?" his father asked.

Darkus thought about it for a while, then shrugged it off. He carried on his sweep of the room, until the flash-light beam struck upon a familiar shape sitting on a shelf. "Look . . ." It was a large jar of *Polish dill pickles*—nearly empty. Darkus ran a gloved finger over the lid and found no dust. "It's recent . . . I'd say within the past twelve hours."

Knightley inspected the container. "At least she's not being mistreated."

Darkus held up the jar and silently cursed himself. So far their foreign investigation had produced little more than a triangle and two jars of pickles. This was pathetic by any standards. He angled the container and shined the penlight through the murky greenish liquid, hoping for a miracle, but finding only a cluster of unappealing, fermented vegetables bobbing around like a school of whales. He balanced the light between his teeth and unscrewed the aluminum lid. A strong aroma of vinegar stung his nostrils. He lowered the jar and quickly went to reseal it when he noticed something on the inside of the lid . . . scratched into the metal with a sharp object—a hair clip, he deduced. He angled the light with his mouth and squinted. The crude engraving showed two words:

It was undoubtedly a message from their housekeeper. Darkus held the illuminated lid for his father to see.

"Vegas . . . a trap." Knightley nodded. "Thank you, my dear Bogna. That's all we need to know."

Suddenly, the jar slipped out of Darkus's hand and smashed into pieces, the pickles squirming in all directions, as—

A blast of white light seared through the open door and window frames, so bright that both Knightleys cowered, half blinded. The light found its way into the building any way it could, penetrating missing roof tiles and holes in the brickwork, turning the entire house into a Halloween jack-o'-lantern.

The Knightleys turned away from the source, only to face

another one blasting through the opposite side of the house, then two more light beams to the left and right.

"What do you want from us?" Knightley shouted out to whoever might be listening. He grabbed Darkus and covered him in the lapels of his coat, maneuvering him toward a back door. Knightley kicked down the door and staggered outside, finding the desert ground turned white hot.

Darkus peered through his fingers to see a ring of steel surrounding the house. Military Humvee all-terrain vehicles were positioned around the building, each with a crew of two and roof-mounted searchlights blazing down on the Knightleys from every angle. Darkus could just make out Irwin, Rufus, and Tilly being held captive by a group of men dressed in black, leaning against one of the vehicles. Amid the dazzling sensory overload, Darkus recalled the phrase "men in black": a term coined by conspiracy theorists to describe government agents who arrived at UFO sites to eliminate evidence, or loose ends—or even witnesses, some claimed.

"Take me to your leader," shouted Knightley.

"They're not aliens, Alan," Irwin called out. "They're government! Far worse!"

"Hands on your heads! Now!" a deep voice commanded.

The Knightleys complied with the request. Several of the searchlights flicked out, leaving a single beam trapping them in its glare.

One of the men in black stepped forward, visible only as a silhouette in military fatigues and a baseball cap, his American accent clipped and aggressive. "What's the purpose of your visit?"

"We're looking for a friend," Darkus answered.

"Have you heard of SO42? The Department of the Unexplained?" Knightley added.

"Is this some kind of joke to you?" the figure shot back.

"I don't think he has heard of them, Dad," said Darkus.

"How about the Combination?" Tilly shouted from the cordon.

"We get crackpots twenty-four-seven every day and twice on Sunday," replied the figure. "They go by all kinds of names."

"I'm a licensed private investigator in the state of California," announced Irwin from beside his son.

"This is Nevada," said the man in black. "We got a tip-off when you crossed state lines, and we've been tracking you ever since."

"A tip-off from whom?" asked Darkus.

"That's classified," the man snapped back.

"The Combination . . . that's who told them," Knightley whispered. "They've outplayed us again."

"So what do we do?" muttered Darkus.

"Take the fight to the enemy," said his father.

"Go to Las Vegas? Even though we know it's a trap?"

"We've always known this was a trap, Doc. It's time to face the music and finish the game."

The man in black instructed his unit: "Detain them. Indefinitely."

Darkus and his dad were frog-marched through the sand to a hulking Humvee troop carrier with two bench seats in the hold. Waiting for them inside were the Bradleys and Tilly, with their wrists and ankles bound with cable ties. An officer trussed the Knightleys' hands and feet too, then manhandled them into the back of the vehicle.

"Well, this is just great," complained Tilly.

"Don't worry," replied Rufus. "They can't hold us for more than twenty-four hours."

"We don't have twenty-four hours," murmured Darkus.

"Quiet," barked an officer as he rifled through the Knightleys' backpacks. Finding no weapons inside, he slung the bags into the back of the hold and slammed the door. The barrel of a heavy lock turned, securing them inside.

A second later the V8 engine rumbled to life, and the Humvee lurched away over the rough terrain, slamming its occupants back and forth.

Knightley leaned forward on his knees and steepled his fingers, entering a state of deep meditation.

"Dad . . . ?" said Darkus, fearing the worst.

"Don't worry, I'm just thinking," Knightley answered. "I estimate our chances of escape at approximately a thousand to one. The other option being almost certain deportation back to Britain—without cracking the Combination. And, most importantly, without Bogna."

150

"A thousand to one . . . ," Irwin repeated. "That's the odds of all five of us escaping, right?"

"Correct," replied Knightley.

"Then how do the odds change if only three of us escape?"

"What are you saying?" asked Knightley.

Darkus chimed in. "I think Irwin is saying that if he and Rufus sacrifice their liberty and remain in custody, our chances of success are significantly increased. Closer to five hundred to one, I'd say."

"I'll take those odds," said Tilly.

Darkus nodded soberly as the Humvee bounced violently over a sand dune.

"What about you?" Knightley asked the Bradleys.

"We're US citizens," replied Irwin. "They can't torture us, they can't deport us. They could keep us holed up for a while, but we've got nothing to hide."

Knightley furrowed his brow. "You'd do that . . . ? For us?"

"Hook me up next time we're in London," said Irwin.

"I'll arrange tea with the Queen," Knightley promised.

"It's cool, Alan." Irwin bumped his pair of bound fists with Knightley's. "You're my 'brother from another mother.'"

Darkus took a moment to deduce what Irwin was saying. "I don't think that's biologically possible," he pointed out, "but it's a wonderful sentiment."

Rufus turned to Knightley Senior and nodded. "That would make you my uncle from another grandmother," he added, perplexed.

Knightley smiled. "I believe you're right, Rufus."

Tilly interjected, "Okay, if you brainiacs have finished working out your family tree, can you help me break us out of here?"

The Knightleys and the Bradleys turned to see Tilly extending her bound feet with almost balletic grace toward her backpack, which was sitting at the end of the hold.

"Hold my hands," she instructed Darkus in the seat beside her. He did so, and she used him as a counterweight to reach even farther toward the end of the vehicle. But it still wasn't enough. "Damn it," she cursed. Then the Humvee hit an almighty bump and threw all of its occupants into the air— before slumping them back in their seats.

Magically, the backpack slid down the briefly inclined vehicle and landed at Tilly's feet.

"Bingo," she said, lifting it with both legs in an impressive abdominal exercise and unzipping the bag with her bound hands. She rummaged around in the compartment before pulling out the hairdryer.

"You Brits really do like to keep up appearances," remarked Irwin, then recoiled as Tilly slid the switch backward and a ten-inch blue flame ignited from the nozzle, transforming the hairdryer into a blowtorch.

She trained the hissing flame on the cable tie at her ankles and melted through it, then turned it on Darkus, who instinctively parted the heels of his hands as she fried the bindings. She handed him the blowtorch and he returned the favor, freeing her. She then released Knightley and arrived at the Bradleys—until Irwin raised his hands and shook his head.

"This is where we say *adios, amigos*. Got to maintain our cover story," Irwin explained. "You guys made a run for it, and we acted like responsible citizens."

"Thanks again," said Darkus, touched.

"Good luck," replied Rufus.

"See you in England," added Irwin.

Knightley and Darkus slung on their backpacks and held Tilly steady as she knelt down and angled the blowtorch on the lock securing the rear door. The lock glowed red, the flame stuttered, low on gas, then the lock barrel fell out and the door swung open.

Outside, the Humvee was steadily climbing a steep sand dune, populated with cactus plants and coarse vegetation.

"Looks . . . prickly," observed Darkus.

"Here goes nothing," said Tilly, then tightened her backpack like a parachutist and dived out of the moving vehicle. "So long, suckers!"

Darkus hesitated, until his dad said, "After you," and pushed him out. Darkus tucked and rolled off into the undergrowth.

Knightley nodded to the Bradleys, snapped a salute, then threw himself out of the Humvee after his young companions.

All three of them made soft landings on the crest of the

dune before rolling downhill out of control, over spiny yucca plants and scrub bushes—which prompted a multitude of imaginative swear words.

Tilly, then Darkus, then Knightley came to rest at the base of the hill, finding themselves inadvertently camouflaged by dust, twigs, and sand. Knightley took a sharp intake of breath as he extracted a particularly large cactus needle from his behind.

"Not exactly the souvenir I was hoping for," he groaned.

A hundred yards above them, the Humvee continued its lumbering progress with the door flapping open and the Bradleys sitting obediently inside.

Darkus brushed off his clothes and looked around. They were surrounded by a high razor-wire fence on all sides. "It would appear our situation remains bleak."

Tilly dug in her backpack, retrieved her hairdryer, switched it on, but got only a sputter of gas and then nothing.

On higher ground, the Humvee's powerful headlights arrived at a checkpoint with several armed guards. The vehicle rumbled to a halt. Seconds later a deafening siren began howling across the desert valley.

"Bleaker by the moment," agreed Knightley.

Several megawatt searchlights began scanning the hills, intermittently casting the landscape in blinding light then darkness, as if alternating between day and night.

"Over there," said Darkus, pointing out a rectangular

white hangar on a nearby access road, before lowering the palm of his hand to indicate "crouch" and tapping his head to indicate "follow me."

Tilly set off into the undergrowth after Darkus, then turned to Knightley and pumped her fist to indicate "hurry up." Knightley returned a thumbs-up and followed them in a low run across the breadth of the hill.

As the searchlights crisscrossed the compound, the trio fell to the ground, ducking under the beams, then covered the last thirty yards to the hangar. Darkus located a single doorway in the wall with a *Restricted* sign on it. But what was the difference? The whole area was restricted. Knightley wasted no time, shoved his shoulder against the door and broke it down.

CHAPTER 15
THE IMPASSE

Inside the hangar it was pitch-black, and the air was eerily still. Darkus felt for his penlight and switched it on, illuminating a small circle around them but not managing to penetrate the darkness beyond. He noted a series of markings on the concrete floor.

Knightley examined a row of shelves containing weapons, ammo, and clay-like blocks of plastic explosive. But no amount of firepower could help them out of their current situation.

Tilly walked nonchalantly into the inky blackness until there was a small clang, followed by an "Ouch!"

Darkus followed the sound with his flashlight beam and found Tilly rubbing her forehead, standing beside a section of metal fuselage.

"What is it?" he asked.

"Looks like a . . . craft of some kind," said Knightley, catching up with them.

"Do you think it's a *real* UFO?" Tilly wondered in awe.

"I don't think so," said Darkus, finding the stars-and-stripes insignia and the words *United States of America.*

"Help me in," ordered Tilly, climbing over the body of the vehicle to grab onto a red handle, which she pulled, causing a hatch to hiss open.

Darkus heard the sound of several Humvees converging outside the hangar, their engines revving.

Knightley hefted Tilly, then Darkus, then himself through the opening into a bubble-shaped cockpit constructed out of Plexiglas viewing windows, with an array of touchscreens for a dashboard.

Darkus ran his hands over the console, finding his way to a joystick controller, while Tilly located a laminated folder with a title on the front: *SEV—Quick Start Guide.*

Knightley strapped himself into a seat behind the other two and watched anxiously.

Outside the hangar, the Humvees began lining up, their searchlights saturating the building.

The man in black's voice bellowed through the PA system. "Come out with your hands in the air—!" He was interrupted by a strange noise.

The hangar doors rolled aside as a large, buggy-like vehicle careened out of the building with a high-pitched whine, before swiveling around on the spot and accelerating up a steep, forty-five-degree sand dune. The cockpit glass was mirrored to reflect heat, and the chassis rested on six sets of independently steering off-road wheels, which gave it the ability to turn, rotate, or reverse in an instant.

Inside the cockpit, Darkus wrestled with the joystick, jerking the vehicle left and right, while Tilly navigated the touchscreens and switched on a cluster of outboard spotlights to illuminate the way.

"I've heard of SUVs . . . but what's an SEV?" demanded Knightley, holding on to his seat as they climbed an impossibly precipitous dune.

"Space Exploration Vehicle," responded Darkus, without taking his eyes off the road. "I imagine it's a relative of the Mars Rover. Experimental, of course."

Two Humvees gave chase up the sharp incline until their wheels lost traction and the vehicles slid backward under their own weight and toppled to the ground in a conjoined hunk of steaming metal.

The whine of the SEV reached an even higher octave as the vehicle picked up speed, gaining traction on the loose rubble and bouncing over the mountainous landscape, its outboard lamps lighting the way as if it were navigating a lunar surface. Two more Humvees swarmed after it. Darkus watched the buggy's spotlights pick out a checkpoint, then he swerved around a terrified guard, rotated one hundred and eighty degrees and took off in the opposite direction, getting air over the crest of a hill.

The vehicle smashed down on the other side, jolting the entire cabin.

"Student drivers," complained Knightley.

"Want to try?" Darkus offered. His father shook his head vigorously.

The SEV descended a near-vertical slope, causing its passengers to flop forward, held in place only by their safety harnesses. A pursuing Humvee soared over the incline after them, then lost control and barrel-rolled past them, its headlights gaping into midair. A second Humvee flew after it like a demolition derby, landing badly and rolling length-wise down the hill behind them, picking up speed.

Darkus glanced at the rearview camera. "We've got company."

Tilly's eyes went wide, seeing the wounded Humvee tumbling like a log toward them, its windows smashing and blowing out with each impact, the headlights rolling wildly, its body panels contorting further with each rotation.

"It appears to be gaining on us," warned Knightley.

Darkus nudged the joystick, pulling a ninety-degree turn and veering out of the way just as the remains of the Humvee hurtled past like an asteroid, coming to rest as a smoking junkyard wreck.

Tilly cross-referenced the screens and pointed through the glass at a fast-approaching razor-wire fence. "I suggest we test the grappling arms."

"The what?" asked Knightley.

Tilly stabbed the screen and two robotic metal arms extended ahead of the cockpit. She traced her finger over a highlighted menu showing a selection of tools. The pincers on the end of the arms retracted and pivoted to allow two circular buzz saws to unfold in their place. The blades spun to life, their serrated teeth whirring at several thousand revolutions per minute.

The robotic arms waved around wildly as the vehicle smashed into the wire fence and the saws severed the chain links, punching a perfect-size hole in the perimeter. The six sets of off-road tires flattened the fence as the SEV trundled off into the desert.

From the compound, the sound of helicopter blades droned to life, slicing through the air as two choppers ascended, dipped their noses, and set off in pursuit.

"Kill the lights," said Tilly.

Darkus switched to an infrared view, then heard a warning sound accompanied by a flashing red battery symbol on the touchscreen. "We're running out of power."

"Already?" demanded Knightley. "It wouldn't last long on Mars or Venus."

"It relies on a solar panel," Darkus pointed out. "But on Earth at 3 a.m., that's not much help."

"It's time to ditch anyway," said Tilly. "They'll be using thermal imagery."

Darkus swerved down a sharp mountain pass that would be impossible for any other vehicle to negotiate. The SEV

160

descended the slope steadily, its treads digging into the soil, churning up dust and bits of vegetation as it went.

He put the buggy into low gear, slowing its progress. "So long, Rover . . ."

Darkus and Tilly released the hatch and it hissed open, letting in the warm desert breeze. One by one, the trio hopped from the slow-moving vehicle, recovering their balance on the slope. They watched as the lonely SEV continued its descent, its robotic arms flailing in the darkness as if it were investigating a foreign planet.

Darkus turned and saw a row of dim caves set in the hillside. "We could shelter there for a few hours."

They scampered across the rough face of the hill and ducked into an opening. Tilly took out her smartphone and, unsurprisingly, discovered the signal bars were empty. Darkus raised his penlight and examined their new quarters. The caves tunneled deep into the hill, with a dusty track leading into the darkness. It was cool and well protected from the unforgiving desert climate. Darkus panned the light over the walls and found a line of handprints that appeared to be painted in red dye, or perhaps blood.

"Native American artwork," he deduced, finding more and more of them, almost like wallpaper, extending into the unknown.

Tilly and Knightley Senior looked around, slightly creeped out.

"Judging by the position of the thumbs and the angle and direction of the handprints," Darkus went on, "the artists began their piece at the other end of this tunnel. Which would suggest that there is another exit . . . somewhere in there." He aimed his weakening flashlight beam into the cavernous passageway.

"Your reasoning is sound," said his father.

They followed the handprints, the penlight picking up primitive patterns and occasional pictures emblazoned on the walls: a dazzling sun, an army of warriors on horseback, and a man falling into space.

Tilly returned to her sullen silence, following behind Darkus and his dad.

After what he estimated to be two miles, Darkus spotted a chink of blue-gray light at the end of the tunnel. It was the pale light of the waning moon. The cave passage opened into a clearing on the other side of the hill from Area 51. The blackened circle of an old bonfire was the only remnant of life, but the ashes had long been scattered by the wind. They looked out over a vista of flat, featureless desert, dotted with cacti and tumbleweeds.

Darkus looked up into the predawn sky and narrowed his eyes, locating a constellation of stars forming a lazy question mark hanging in space. "That's the Big Dipper, also known as Ursa Major," he explained.

"Which makes that the Little Dipper," added Knightley Senior, pointing to a smaller constellation with a similar shape. "Ursa Minor."

Darkus took his penlight and held it aloft like a ruler, forming an imaginary line between the top two stars of the Big Dipper and the top star of the Little Dipper—which appeared to shine a little brighter than the rest. "Which makes that the North Star. Due north," Darkus concluded.

"Which means Las Vegas is thatta way," confirmed his father, pointing southward into the gloom. The geography appeared to unfold, revealing the full scope of the task ahead. "We must cover as much ground as possible before the sun comes up. The heat will slow our progress considerably, and we don't have the benefit of fresh drinking water."

"Before we go any farther . . . I have a question," Tilly interjected, causing the Knightleys to snap out of their steel-trap minds for a moment. "It's for *you*, Alan."

"Fire away," he responded calmly.

Darkus watched, sensing this was the question that had hung over Tilly ever since they left Los Angeles: the megaton bomb that had been hurtling toward them, ready to set off a chain reaction and detonate the fragile alliance of this holy detective trinity. Darkus felt his catastrophizer clatter to life, reacting to the tension in the air.

Knightley did his best to disguise his own anxiety, but it was a losing battle.

163

"Why was my mother communicating with Underwood before her death . . . ?" Tilly demanded.

"That's ridiculous," Knightley countered.

"*Why?*" she repeated.

"Your mother was my assistant. She worked for me. We were trying to locate Underwood—"

"*Stop lying to me!!!!*" she screamed, and her yell echoed across the canyons. Her face flushed red with rage. "My mother communicated with Underwood even after he was a wanted man—even after he was on the run for the murder of that boy."

Darkus recalled the case history. Underwood: the renowned child psychologist; wanted in connection with the death of one of his young patients.

"She communicated with Underwood right up until her death," Tilly insisted. "Arranging meetings, exchanging coded messages. You know how I know? Because I read the e-mails. They were on Underwood's hard drive." Tilly shook the smartphone at him, even though at this point it was a useless brick. "What power did he have over her? Why did she talk to Underwood, only for him to turn around and have her killed?"

Knightley shook his head, massaging his temples. "I can't tell you," he pleaded, though it wasn't clear whether he didn't know, or he couldn't say.

"I don't know everything. *Yet,*" Tilly accused him. "I'll have to wait for a few more hours and a decent Wi-Fi signal.

But I *do* know you've been *lying* to me. All along—!" She lunged at Knightley Senior, who held her off with one hand. She managed to push him back a few steps. "The truth this time. No more lies. I deserve that." She grabbed him by the lapels, breathless.

"I—I . . ." Knightley's eyes rolled back.

"No!" she ordered. "Don't check out on me. Don't even think about it—!" she begged, shaking Knightley violently as the man's knees buckled and he began to descend into one of his episodes.

"Dad!!" Darkus ran to catch him as he fell.

Knightley collapsed into the dust, his head narrowly missing a rock. Darkus slumped next to him, brushing the sand from his father's face and hair, then carefully raising his closed lids. The pupils were fixed and dilated. Knightley's nostrils continued to flare as his chest heaved and sank at regular intervals.

"That no-good sonofa—" Tilly aimed a kick at Knightley's ribs with the hope of bringing him back to life, but Darkus blocked her foot with the blade of his forearm, as he'd learned from his father's preferred martial art, Wing Chun—deflecting her energy away. Tilly rebounded and withdrew, looking quietly impressed by her stepbrother's reaction. Then she continued her verbal assault regardless. "He doesn't care about anybody except himself. He doesn't care about *you*. He *definitely* doesn't care about me. He probably couldn't care less about what happened to your dog either."

Darkus let the accusation hang in the air, not wishing to give it any power—or to contemplate the fact that it might actually contain a grain of truth.

Tilly collected herself. "I'm sorry. That was a low blow."

"Your personal vendetta against my dad doesn't help our current predicament," said Darkus, then checked his father's pulse and looked around the wasteland, crestfallen. "He's having one of his episodes, and we could die out here. Without Bogna. Without any answers. Without anything but heat, dust, and death."

The edge of the rising sun began to bleed across the horizon, grotesquely enlarged, like an object of beauty and an agent of destruction all at once. Soaring over it was the foreboding shape of a vulture, its feathers ragged: a bad omen; a harbinger of doom. "We'll be lucky if they even find our bones. Then who wins?" Darkus asked her. "The Combination, that's who. Game, set, and match."

Tilly stared at her feet remorsefully, then dug into her backpack and pulled out three silver packets. "Well, I did borrow these. From the Rover." She handed one to Darkus. It had a NASA logo on it. "They're called MREs," she explained. "Meals Ready to Eat. Astronaut food. One for each of us. And we don't need a microwave to heat them up."

"Good work. We'll save them for the journey."

"To Las Vegas?" she protested.

"Dad was right. It's time to complete the game."

"Okay, Einstein," she piped up. "How do we travel a

166

hundred miles in over-one-hundred-degree heat?" She pointed to Knightley Senior. "My vote is to leave him here."

"I'm not leaving him," insisted Darkus, casting his eye over the plains.

They sat in defeated silence for close to an hour, watching the vulture circle ever closer, revealing its giant, prehistoric wingspan, intermittently blocking out the sun, until it flew directly over them.

Darkus scanned the horizon hopelessly, feeling the roof of his mouth already parched and hollow, like the cracked surface under his shoes.

Then something caught his eye.

A *glint*. In fact, there were *two* glints, side by side. Darkus reached into his pocket and unfolded a pair of mini binoculars, racking the focus wheel until he arrived at a blobby shape. Two blobs, one behind the other. Darkus rubbed his eyes for a moment.

"I must be seeing things. A mirage or something . . . ," he muttered.

"What is it?" Tilly demanded.

Darkus pressed his face to the eyecups, seeing something out of a Wild West movie: two burly men in cowboy hats and ponchos, riding two aging stallions in a very amateurish fashion. The lead rider also held a pair of binoculars to his face, which appeared to be trained directly on Darkus. Darkus's and the rider's binoculars met, observing each other, then a pudgy hand was raised and waved enthusiastically.

"I *have* to be seeing things . . . ," Darkus murmured, then looked again.

The rider removed his cowboy hat and pointed at his heavily perspiring face, mouthing something that appeared to be . . . "*It's me.*"

"Uncle Bill!" Darkus could hardly believe his eyes. "It's Uncle Bill!"

Tilly snatched the binoculars and confirmed it, breaking into a wide smile. Through the lenses, Bill awkwardly swiveled in his saddle, nearly losing his balance, then grabbed onto the reins and pointed to his partner on the horse behind. It was none other than Dougal Billoch, Bill's brother. (Dougal was allegedly the younger brother, although the two looked like identical twins.) Both were sweating buckets, waving their arms and legs as they coaxed their horses through the desert. The stallions appeared indifferent to the riders' demands, but within an hour—and after Bill briefly lost the saddle entirely and found himself riding underneath the horse—the two Scotsmen came to the rescue.

CHAPTER 16
RIDERS ON THE STORM

Untangling themselves from their reins, stirrups, and cinches, the two brothers unceremoniously dismounted, clumping to the ground. Their stallions whinnied, then relieved themselves on the remnants of the bonfire. Darkus realized the Scotsmen had taken their mission seriously, outfitting themselves in authentic Western attire, complete with cowboy boots and spurs. Darkus even caught a glimpse of a Colt .45 revolver tucked into a leather holster strapped around Bill's generous hip.

"Aye, Doc, ye weren't easy to find—I see Alan's had a bottle o' vino collapso." Bill peeled off his hat and swigged from a hefty hip flask fashioned out of animal skin. The liquid caused him to crank his neck, waggle both his chins, then splutter violently. "Ay, *caramba!* Sorry, ye must be spittin' feathers yerselves." He went to offer it around before coming to his senses. "On second thought, have one o' these instead." He offered the teens a plastic sport bottle of Highland Spring water each, which they gulped in short drafts.

Darkus knelt by his dad, who was currently propped unconscious in the shade at the entrance to the caves. He gently drip-fed water into his father's mouth. Knightley's swallow reflex activated, his eyelids fluttered, and he appeared to smile gratefully for a moment before returning to his trancelike state.

"How *did* you find us?" Darkus asked the Scotsmen.

Bill removed a cigar from the corner of his mouth and pointed it at the chain around Knightley's neck. "Miss Khan took the liberty o' concealing a homing device inside that there Saint Christopher medal."

Darkus read the inscription again: *Saint Christopher Protect Us*. More like *Miss Khan Protect Us*, for it was his faithful science teacher who had saved them from certain death in the desert. Darkus made a silent promise to hand in his homework on time, every time, from now on.

"We also brought some of these," announced Dougal, digging in his poncho and pulling out a packet of chocolate digestive biscuits. "A taste o' home. They're a wee bit melted, ah'm afraid," he admitted. "And the other packet went missin'." He shot an accusing glance at his big brother, who looked away, ashamed.

"Did you find out anything more before you left?" inquired Darkus.

"Not a Scooby," replied Bill. "Clorr Entertainment is

sewn up tight as a fankle. We cannot work out who they are or where to find 'em. It's all smoke and mirrors, farts 'n' deception." Bill's horse whinnied accusingly from the mouth of the cave. "Haud yer wheesht!" the Scotsman shouted back.

"What about Underwood?" said Tilly.

"Still clammed up, sleepin' like a bubby," Bill responded. "Under round-the-clock supervision. He's not goin' anywhere, I can guarantee ye that. How 'bout ye?"

"Time is short," said Darkus. "I'll fill you in on the way." He packed the MRE rations into Bill's saddlebags, then glanced at the sun, which was rising steadily and gaining in intensity.

"On the way where?" asked Bill.

"Las Vegas," said Tilly.

"We believe that's where Bogna is being held," explained Darkus.

Bill's clammy face broke into a cigar-chomping grin. "Belter!"

After a lot of heaving and struggling, and the horse bolting more than once, Knightley Senior was loaded facedown, doubled over the back of Dougal's steed. His unconscious body was secured with a thick leather belt and a blanket to protect him from the sun, causing Knightley to resemble a captured outlaw from the Old West being transported to

171

the sheriff's office, "dead or alive"—it was hard to tell which.

Darkus and Tilly climbed aboard Uncle Bill's horse, sitting one behind the other as if it were a three-seat tandem bicycle: Tilly holding on to Darkus, who spread his arms wide to hold on to Bill.

Following several minutes of adjusting, readjusting, cinching, cajoling, and one final adjustment, Bill shouted, "Yah!!" But the horse didn't budge an inch. Bill shifted in his saddle as if he was trying to kick-start a motorbike. "Boo-yaaah!" Bill deliberated for a moment. "Giddyup, ye stinky hogbeast!"

The horse took off at a gallop with Bill, Darkus, and Tilly holding on for dear life, leaving a trail of billowing dust in their wake.

"Yah!! Yah!!"

A full five minutes later, Dougal was still coaxing his stallion into action, until he dropped the reins and collapsed forward with exhaustion—at which point the animal unexpectedly took off after the others, with Dougal clinging to its neck and Knightley's limp body flopping and waving from behind the saddle.

The unlikely posse of riders made surprisingly good progress through the desert flats, navigating deep red canyons and dry riverbeds, progressing into the "bad-lands": dense, arid mountain ranges so gnarled and eroded by wind and rain that they were near impossible to traverse. Still the horses pressed on, carrying their motley cargo under the granite-blue skies, Tilly wearing a creased sun hat and Darkus uncrumpling a straw trilby that he'd bought at Heathrow. After the group had spent the better part of the day on horseback with only the occasional rest stop, the shadows grew longer as the sun sank in the western sky. The badlands became more ominous than ever, their jagged gouge marks darkening as dusk threatened to fall.

"Are we there yet?" demanded Tilly.

Uncle Bill didn't answer. Darkus peered around the Scotsman's massive torso to find he'd fallen asleep at the reins, his cowboy hat tipped forward to shade him from the light.

Darkus glanced at the position of the sun. "I estimate we're over halfway."

Tilly turned to Dougal's stallion trotting beside them, then examined Knightley Senior's body, still draped unconscious over its hindquarters, occasionally being swished in the face by the horse's tail. "He'll wish he never woke up once I'm done with him," she said menacingly. "I've been brushing up on my 'enhanced interrogation' techniques."

Darkus realized it was easier to talk to her without looking her in the eye. "We need to stay focused on the case, for all our sakes," he advised.

"You stay focused on your case," she warned. "I'll stay focused on mine."

"Tilly . . ." He tried to word his next sentence carefully, realizing his stepsister needed something more from him and his dad—more than finding Bogna; more than the dangerous thrill of playing a game with the Combination. She needed answers. Darkus took a deep breath, then confessed: "Dad said something when we were in LA. I was half asleep at the time, but I heard him say . . . that there was something I *needed to know*."

Darkus felt Tilly's body flinch behind him on the horse. Her fingers tensed up, almost digging into his waist. He could feel her anger as an electrical charge, running from her hands into his body like a pair of cattle prods.

"What do you mean?" she demanded. "*What was it?*"

Darkus paused. "I don't exactly know."

He felt her whole body sag behind him, as if the disappointment was too much to bear.

"Great, *Dorkus*, that's really helpful,' she snapped, then silently winced—acknowledging that the use of that name for her loyal stepbrother was a new low, even for her.

"What I'm saying is . . . ," Darkus went on, undeterred, "I think Dad *does* know more about how your mom died than he's told you. And I promise, one way or another, we'll get to the truth."

Tilly swallowed, finding it hard to say: "Thanks."

"We're your family too, Tilly. Remember that."

174

She nodded slowly, and Darkus thought he felt her grip gently tighten just a little, almost becoming a hug— impossible as it might have been to believe.

"I'm going to get some shut-eye," she said, putting on a brave face, then yawning.

"Okay," Darkus replied, and felt her head lower onto his shoulder.

The horses trooped on as the sun went down and dusk cast a swath of blue light over the proceedings.

In the distance, Darkus saw something that looked like a shooting star. Then another, and another. They were traveling horizontally in twinned clusters—until he realized they were the streaks of headlights from passing cars.

"Uncle Bill . . ." He roused the Scotsman from his slumber.

"Aye." Bill adjusted his cowboy hat and poncho.

"I think it's civilization," said Darkus, seeing a neon shroud in the southern sky.

The horses tentatively approached a fast-moving expressway beating its own path through the desert, causing the animals to whinny and stomp their hooves at the speeding vehicles.

"No, Doc," replied Bill with a smile. "It's *Sin City* . . ."

For beyond the road was a far greater light show. Off in the distance, nestled in a vast dust bowl, was a humming oasis of neon, dotted with palm trees and vertical beams strafing the heavens. In the center was a dazzling skyline of every conceivable shape, style, and color—completely man-made and completely alien. All wrapped in an alluring, golden glow.

"Welcome to Las Vegas . . ."

CHAPTER 17
THE STRIP

Bill and Dougal first returned the two valiant steeds to their surprised-looking owner at a local ranch off the highway.

"Found what you folks were lookin' for?" drawled the genuine cowboy, cocking his hat as Bill unstrapped the body that was tied to the back of Dougal's horse.

"Aw, this mucker?" replied Bill, slapping Knightley's unconscious behind. "He's an old pal. Still got some lookin' to do, but we won't be needing any horsies where we're going."

Bill's steed stomped its hooves and whinnied loudly in his direction.

"Same to ye!" the Scotsman replied.

"Won't be needin' this getup either," added Dougal as the two brothers wriggled out of their cowboy hats, ponchos, and chaps, stripping down to their boots and matching tartan undergarments.

The spectacle was fortuitously obscured by an arriving yellow cab, which had been hailed to take the team into town.

"That's not a dead body, is it?" asked the driver, pointing at Knightley's limp form leaning against a hitching post.

"Just sleepin' off a big night," explained Bill, who emerged with Dougal, both having changed into color-coordinated red-and-green leisure suits, while retaining their cowboy boots.

"Good, 'cause that'd be extra," replied the cabbie, perfectly serious.

Bill hoisted Knightley up by his armpits while his brother took hold of the feet. "Keep yer end up, Dougal! To me!"

The Scotsmen loaded Knightley into the accommodating trunk, alongside their luggage, then Bill rode shotgun and Dougal joined the teens in the backseat as the cab pulled away.

The dark desert highway soon made way for a grid of brightly lit streets, lined with palm trees and sweltering with heat, as they closed in on the pulsing center of "Sin City."

Darkus had informed Bill of the word *Trap* next to the word *Vegas* in Bogna's message. But, throughout history, Las Vegas had always been a trap: it was a make-believe El Dorado, a fairy tale built by Italian-American mobsters to relieve people of their hard-earned money, with extravagant hotels, casinos, card tables, and cabaret shows. Then the city passed into the hands of other gangsters, with names like Bugsy, Moe, and Lucky—though some weren't lucky enough to dodge a hit man's bullet. And more recently, Las

Vegas had fallen into the hands of corporations and big businessmen, who re-created it as a family mega-resort, with themed hotels complete with costumed employees, superstar concerts, boxing matches, DJs, and nightclubs. "Gambling" was now known as "gaming." Instead of Sin City, these days Las Vegas preferred to be known as the Entertainment Capital of the World.

And Darkus could see why. Pressing on through the city limits, they saw multiple beacons each seeking their attention, towering buildings of all imaginable shapes, elaborate light shows in every direction. They passed a vast electricity substation that took up an entire city block. The town was glowing with power, heat, and color. As they drove along Las Vegas Boulevard, they saw tourists filling the streets alongside caped superheroes, knights in suits of armor, pirates, and Roman emperors. Street promoters, or "hawkers," fanned flyers through their fingers and flicked them to gain attention before handing them out to advertise every conceivable entertainment. This was a place of extreme fantasy. Where inhibitions were left at home and indulgence ran rampant. It was a city of games and deception.

If the Combination were planning their ultimate play, there was no better place to do it than here.

Darkus's phone began buzzing incessantly, picking up a cell signal for the first time in some twenty hours. The screen flashed on with eleven missed calls, all tagged *Mum*.

179

Feeling too guilt-ridden to check his voice mail, Darkus pocketed the phone and decided to wait until they'd found a room for the night. It may not have been the most logical decision, but logic appeared to feature less and less in his mind these days. Perhaps that was part of growing up. He justified his reluctance to call her by reasoning that it was the early hours of the morning in the UK, though it was evening in the western US. He resolved to get in touch before she had breakfast on her side of the world. Then she would receive his full and humble confession of where he was and how he'd gotten there.

Meanwhile, Tilly obsessively checked her own phone signal, watching the timer enter its final hour: 00:59:46—45—44 . . .

"This is the center of the action," the driver announced. "The Las Vegas Strip. Where to now?"

Bill looked to Darkus and Tilly.

"I don't know . . . yet," admitted Darkus, searching his detective instincts but coming up blank. "Just drive."

Outside the cab, hotels started popping up as if out of nowhere. First the Stratosphere Casino, Hotel & Tower, its space needle extending up into the sky like a rocket on a launchpad, with a rotating observation deck a thousand feet up, and a roller coaster ride above that. Then Circus Circus, with its big-top-shaped building and a giant clown beckoning customers inside. Darkus, Tilly, and the Billochs craned their necks to see each subsequent attraction, their faces painted in a kaleidoscope of color, while Knightley simply snored from the trunk.

Next was Treasure Island, with its own pirate ship docked in a man-made bay outside the hotel. Then the more upmarket Venetian hotel, with Italian-inspired architecture and water fountains leaping into the sky to music. (The driver told them that imitation gondolas cruised along imitation Venice canals inside the shopping mall.) They continued past the faux-Roman columns of Caesar's Palace, then the Paris Las Vegas hotel, with its absurd half-scale replica of the Eiffel Tower—which the driver informed them was intended to be a full-scale replica, but it would have obstructed air traffic.

"Wait a second . . ." Darkus stopped him. "What's that?" He pointed through the windshield to a giant reflective glass shape against the skyline.

"That's the newest development on the strip," replied the driver. "It's called the Egyptian Hotel and Casino."

As they got closer, the other buildings seemed to make way to reveal the Egyptian's true dimensions: it was a massive *pyramid*. Darkus did a double take. The pyramid was some forty floors high, made up entirely of mirrored glass, its walls leaning in toward the apex.

"That's where we'll be staying," said Darkus decisively.

The pyramid shape scribbled on the notepad in Survival Town was too specific to be an accident. And finding one in Las Vegas was too lucky to be chance. And besides, Darkus had learned from his father: never succumb to the luxury of coincidence. Tilly looked at him and nodded her agreement.

The cab pulled into the forecourt of the Egyptian and two bellhops in pharaoh headdresses, robes, and sandals jogged over to open the doors. The Billochs were helped out of their seats, followed by Darkus and Tilly. Upon opening the trunk, the bellhops paused, finding an unconscious Knightley Senior among the bags.

"Don't worry, we'll take that one," Bill told them, taking hold of Knightley's upper body before dropping him again as a passing hawker flicked a flyer and handed it to him.

"What's that?" asked Darkus.

"No idea, Doc, but it could be vital evidence." Bill tucked the flyer into an inside pocket and returned to lugging Knightley.

Darkus gave the cabbie a tip, then accompanied Tilly through the grand entrance underneath a towering sphinx, carved out of stone, with an animal's body and a human head staring mysteriously into the night sky. The pair proceeded through a set of dramatic columns into a vast atrium with an open-plan lobby in the center of the pyramid. The walls extended upward at inverted angles, each story containing rows of rooms, like cubicles in a giant, triangular beehive. Wide escalators took tourists gliding up from the ground floor to the shopping mall and food court. It took several seconds for Darkus to get his bearings before he approached the reception desk, which appeared to be over fifty yards long, with some twenty-five receptionists all taking reservations. Darkus went to the first one available and introduced himself.

"The name's Knightley. We don't have a reservation, but my father is currently suffering a narcoleptic episode and we're in need of a room for the night."

"A narco-what?" inquired the receptionist, tilting her head.

Darkus glanced across the foyer to the Billoch brothers, who were struggling with Knightley's body, their cowboy boots skittering on the marble floor.

"Make that two rooms," Darkus added, then turned back to the receptionist and channeled his father's wit and charm. "You see, Dad was on assignment with POTUS . . . that stands for the president of the United States," he confided.

"Oh, my . . . ," warbled the receptionist.

Moments later, Darkus tapped Tilly on the shoulder and directed her to the elevators, which ran up the inside of the walls at a precipitous angle.

"So they had a room?" she asked.

"Only the presidential suite," explained Darkus, motioning to a convoy of bellhops in his wake.

She held up her hand to high-five him, then they fist-bumped and led the convoy into a glass elevator.

"Hold on." Darkus hesitated—the wheels of his investigative mind turning. "Tilly, you get everyone settled. I have a few preliminary inquiries to carry out."

"Need help?" she offered.

He shook his head and stepped back into the lobby. "Keep an eye on Dad, and keep your phone on."

"Duh," she responded, glancing at the ever-present timer on her home screen.

Uncle Bill nodded, impressed. "Aye, he's a chip off the old block, that Doc," the Scotsman panted as he and his brother carried Knightley into the elevator lengthwise. "Watch 'is feet, Dougal!" he snapped as the doors closed and the glass pod began rising up the pyramid wall at a thirty-nine-degree angle. "Oh, mah tottie scones," Bill exclaimed as the ground fell away.

Darkus watched his friends rise into the heavens, then returned to the long check-in desk and approached the receptionist again.

CHAPTER 18
WHAT HAPPENS IN VEGAS

"Master Knightley, how can I be of excellent service?" the receptionist asked.

"Well, we're supposed to be meeting a friend here. Her name is Bogna Rejesz." He spelled the name out carefully. "Do you have a reservation under that name?"

Darkus knew it was a long shot, but sometimes long shots were all a detective had—and this city was built on gambles.

"Well, we wouldn't normally give out that kind of information," said the receptionist, "but seeing as your dad's working with the president and all . . . ," she whispered, typing a command into her keyboard. She pursed her rouged lips and shook her head. "I apologize, but there's nobody here by that name."

Darkus nodded: he thought as much. He paused for a moment, sifting through the other possibilities. "How about *Clorr Entertainment?*" Darkus spelled out the company name clearly. "Anything under that name?"

The receptionist obliged by keying in another command, then she made a glum face. "Sorry, honey, we don't have any reservations under that name either." She rested her fingers on the keyboard and glanced at the screen, before brightening. "Oh, wait. We do have a Miss Pam Clorr staying with us. Might that help?"

Darkus cocked his head, taking in the name. "Pam Clorr . . . yes, that might help. Would you be so kind as to tell me which room she's in?"

"Well, I really shouldn't . . . but you have such a charming accent."

Darkus blushed deeply. "It would be much appreciated, yes-yes."

"It's room thirteen-oh-one. On the thirteenth floor." She added pleasantly, "You know, some hotels in Vegas don't even have a thirteenth floor. It's considered bad luck. But we're not superstitious here at the Egyptian."

"Thank you, ma'am," replied Darkus. "You've been extremely helpful."

He thought about tipping her a few dollars, then concluded it might not be appropriate. He would consult his father on the finer points of tipping versus bribery once he woke up.

Darkus turned away from the reception desk—then stopped dead: seeing a familiar figure striding across the atrium, her stiletto heels clicking on the marble in perfect time with her swiveling hips. Darkus's catastrophizer began pounding between his ears as he examined her blond hair and striking face, compared it against his mental database, checked again to make sure, then identified her as . . . *Chloe Jaeger*: the murder suspect from their first investigation, assistant to literary agent Bram Beecham, whom she'd killed in cold blood in order to conceal their involvement with the Combination and its sinister self-help book, *The Code*. Chloe had also kidnapped Darkus and Tilly in the deserted tunnels of London's Down Street Tube station, before Tilly outwitted her with one of Miss Khan's early prototypes. Chloe's boss, Underwood, had subsequently fallen under a Tube train—only to reappear very much alive in Harley Street a matter of days ago. Chloe, on the other hand, was *never* apprehended—only to show up here, now, at the Egyptian Hotel.

Coincidence? Impossible, concluded Darkus. Chloe was here on the orders of the Combination. But what was the reason for the game? Why had the Knightleys been lured across the world? To become the victims of a simple murder plot? The Combination could have done that at home. If this was a trap—what was the desired result?

Darkus didn't move a muscle, using the line of tourists at reception as cover, tracking Chloe with his eyes. She was dressed in a fashionable jacket, blouse, and skirt ensemble, as if she were attending a business event. Without even glancing in his direction, she walked to an elevator on the opposite wall, entered it, selected a button, and the doors closed. Darkus crossed the lobby in haste, watching as the pod sped up the incline at thirty-nine degrees. He could just make out her slim figure through the glass as the elevator slowed, reaching her floor. Darkus scanned the inverted wall and made a brief calculation of the number of stories. She had stepped out onto the *thirteenth floor*. *Another* coincidence? The line of reasoning was becoming clearer. Had Chloe adopted the name "Pam Clorr"? Was she responsible for snatching Bogna? Each story of the pyramid opened out onto the lobby area, so Darkus would be able to see which direction she took. He watched and waited, squinting up at the rows of rooms, but there was no sign of her. She'd exited the elevator, then simply vanished. Maybe there *was* something strange about the thirteenth floor?

Darkus felt an ache from craning his neck, and looked back down, hardly believing what he'd just witnessed. His catastrophizer drummed insistently in the back of his head. Something was wrong here. Very wrong. The words "Vegas" and "Trap" echoed around his cranium, bouncing through the corridors of his deductive mind. Going to the thirteenth floor alone would be suicide. He would have to report back to Tilly and Uncle Bill and work out a plan of action, but first he wanted to complete his reconnaissance of the hotel while Chloe was safely out of play in her room.

He continued past the twenty-five receptionists, under a cluster of palm trees, past more haunted-looking sphinxes sitting on their beast-like haunches, overseeing the proceedings. The stone walls were etched with hieroglyphs, underlit for maximum effect. Knowing something of ancient Egyptian script, Darkus recognized no genuine logic or sense to any of the inscriptions.

He moved through the bustle of tourists, many in shorts with cameras slung around their necks, then passed into the casino area, flanked by several dense rows of digital slot machines, blaring with noise and color. The word "jackpot" flashed from every direction. Men and women of all ages and descriptions were sitting on high-backed stools, hunched over the machines, punching the illuminated buttons, prompting a cacophony of chirping and burping noises as the screens flickered with revolving symbols, before—very occasionally—spewing coins into the plastic cups of the waiting gamblers. The cherries, lemons, oranges, bells, and number signs on the displays were their own sort of hieroglyphs: symbols of greed rather than hope. The gamblers watched intently, waiting for the right combination of signs to appear. It was a game of chance, not skill. As a detective, Darkus could not fathom relying on luck alone: there was no honor to it; no competitive spirit; just a blind belief in murky fate. Many of the gamblers' faces were desperate, obsessed, their jaws slack, their eyes vacant.

Being underage, Darkus knew that he wasn't permitted to do anything more than walk through the gaming area. He wasn't even allowed to pause. He could explain that he was lost, looking for his parents, or seeking refreshments, but if he lingered near any of the machines, he would be escorted out by members of the ever-present security staff, who were dressed in black, standing at vantage points around the room. Noting the casino guards watching him, Darkus walked farther into the bowels of the pyramid, where the slot machines receded to reveal a luxurious cocoon-like space in the center of the building. This inner sanctum contained semicircular blackjack tables covered in green felt, with dealers in crisp white shirts and vests dispensing cards, and players arranging them into feathered spreads alongside stacks of disc-shaped gaming chips. The chips doubled for currency and would be exchanged for hard cash at the end of the game—whatever time of day or night. Vegas never slept. In fact, it was rumored the hotels pumped pure oxygen into the rooms to keep guests awake and alert—able to gamble more and consume more. Food and drink was on hand twenty-four hours a day. The shopping mall provided retail therapy when needed. The casinos were dimly lit and designed like labyrinths, their red walls curving smoothly into infinity, so it was nearly impossible to find an exit without stumbling into another game. There were no windows, no clocks. Even the frenzied, garish pattern of the carpet was designed to disorient. It was a perfectly sealed, vacuum-packed world with everything a visitor could wish for—and no obvious way out.

The inner sanctum was for the serious players, known as

"whales" or "high rollers"; often well dressed, well groomed, able to win or lose hundreds of thousands, or even millions, with the throw of a die or a winning hand. The casinos gave them hotel suites free of charge, knowing how much they would blow at the gambling tables. The games were conducted using a series of cryptic phrases.

"Care for another one?" the dealer asked.

"Hit me."

The dealer dealt a card.

The player turned it over. "*Three of a kind.*" He laid out three kings: clubs, hearts, and diamonds.

Another dealer shuffled his cards, causing them to virtually float from one hand to the other. "Who's feeling lucky? Remember: what happens in Vegas *stays* in Vegas."

Nearby, a roulette wheel spun, the red and black numbers whirling in the opposite direction to the roulette ball, until the ball sank into a pocket and went for a ride, deciding the gamblers' fate. Elsewhere, Darkus watched a pair of dice tumble across a basin-shaped craps table, coming to rest on two sixes, known as "boxcars." A whoop went up from the winning player, who was dressed in a dark suit, a Spanish gaucho hat pulled low over his face and a ponytail draping down his back: a high roller, for sure.

Darkus did a double take. This player was familiar to him: that hat, shading a goatee beard. He looked again, not believing his eyes: it was *Mr. Presto* . . . Chloe's partner in crime, part-time illusionist, full-time Combination agent.

Darkus's heart beat in his throat as he looked away and kept walking for fear of being recognized. The catastrophizer whirled and clicked like a roulette wheel, alternating between red and black. So the Combination *was* here—in force. And Darkus and his father (not to mention Tilly and the Billochs) were in a world of high-stakes trouble. Darkus sneaked a final glance at Presto as the villain collected his winnings—no doubt won through deception with a set of loaded dice, weighted perfectly to land exactly as he wanted them to.

Darkus searched for a way out of this house of games. He had to get back to Tilly and Uncle Bill before they happened upon the Combination themselves. He tried to retrace his steps, but found the scenery repeating itself: a maze of identical gambling tables, identical rows of slot machines. If he wasn't careful, he could easily find himself face-to-face with Presto again. Darkus stopped in his tracks and tried a different approach: he licked his finger and held it high above his head, screening out the cool gusts from the air-conditioners and instead detecting a slight variation in air pressure, which had to be coming from the open-plan lobby area. He followed his instinct and quickly found himself back at the reception desk. He was heading for the elevators when an even more familiar voice boomed through the forecourt.

"This is phen-o-menal! Let's paar-taaay!"

Darkus spun, seeing a long, stretch Hummer limo pulling

into pole position as one of its passengers rocked and swayed with the top half of his body protruding from the sunroof. Despite it being dark outside, the passenger was wearing a Hawaiian shirt and wraparound sunglasses. Darkus rubbed his eyes.

Incredibly, it was his stepfather: *Clive*.

CHAPTER 19
ALL ROADS CONVERGE

Darkus momentarily forgot the whole investigation as he watched Clive gyrate out of the top of the Hummer limo, until another passenger forcibly pulled him back into the cabin in an attempt to calm him down.

"Hey, Jax, watch the footwear! They're box fresh," he bellowed through the opening.

A team of headdress-wearing bellhops descended on the limo and opened the rear doors to usher out Clive—in Adidas long shorts and brilliant white sneakers—followed by Darkus's mom, Jackie, in a tasteful khaki ensemble.

Darkus stood rooted to the spot.

"I l-oove it already!" declared Clive, peering through his shades.

"Isn't it a bit . . ." Jackie looked for the word. "Flashy?" She glanced around, bewildered, as their bags were carted into the lobby.

"I'll tell you what it is, dear. It's *free!*" Clive yanked Jackie's hand, leading her toward the reception desk, until he came to a stuttering halt, raising his sunglasses in disbelief. "Wait a mo-ment. Do my beer goggles deceive me?"

"Er, hello, Mom. Clive," Darkus announced, standing before them in the foyer.

"Doc!" His mother ran and grabbed him in a warm embrace. "What on earth are you doing here?"

Darkus returned the hug before pulling away, checking his peripheral vision for suspects, all too aware of the circumstances of his presence and the need to keep his mother as far away from those circumstances as possible. "I'm here with Dad and Tilly. What are *you* doing here?"

"I left about a dozen messages on your phone. I thought you must have switched it off. It was a last-minute thing. Clive's producers flew him out here . . . plus one." She gestured meekly to herself. "To say thanks for being such a hit in the ratings."

"That's right," replied Clive, sticking his nose in the air. "And the last thing I expected was your ugly mug to greet me." He glowered at Darkus, with no attempt to disguise his irritation. "This was supposed to be an exclusive, exotic getaway for your mother and me. First-class, five-star, hot towels, and chocolates on the pillow. All expenses paid. A getaway from the likes of you and my reprobate daughter."

"Clive!" Jackie snapped.

Clive frowned for a second, then shrugged off any trace of guilt, enjoying his newfound good fortune. "Well, it's the

195

truth, Jax. Deal with it. If you're not able to enjoy the fruits of my new career, that's your loss."

"We'll discuss this later," she replied, disgusted. "Are you all okay?" she questioned Darkus. "Is Bogna *here* somewhere?"

"I'll tell you everything when I have a solution to the facts," Darkus assured her. "First . . . Clive, I must ask you one urgent question."

Clive kept cranking his head left and right to admire the majesty of the pyramid and the bevy of females strolling past in Cleopatra robes. "Across the line . . . ," he murmured his *Wheel Spin* catchphrase to himself, until—

Darkus swiftly prodded him in his solar plexus: the soft collection of nerves in the center of the upper abdomen.

"Ouch!" yapped Clive, perhaps remembering that Darkus had used this tactic on him once before—that time in a life-or-death situation. "Yessss . . . ?" Clive hissed, rubbing his painful midsection and looking down at his stepson.

"What's the name of the production company that paid for this 'all-expenses-paid' getaway?" demanded Darkus.

"*Clorr*. Clorr Entertainment. Duh! They hired me for the show. They pay the bills. They run the whole gig." Clive returned his attention to the plush surroundings. "We've entered the *Winner's Circle* now, Jax. Come on, babes, I'm a lover not a fighter. Let's play nice and check out the suite. I bet it's spec-tacular!"

Darkus felt his catastrophizer flick through the gears as he processed this latest revelation. So a pattern was forming—and it was not an encouraging one. The Combination's web had expanded dramatically, orchestrating Clive's newfound success, weaving itself even deeper into Darkus's life and threatening to ensnare everyone around him.

"Clive, let me look into your eyes," Darkus demanded.

"What is this? My annual checkup?" he complained. "What do you want me to do next? Cough?"

"Just do as he says," Jackie ordered her husband.

"Okay, dear." Clive knelt as if he was meeting royalty, then Darkus used a thumb and forefinger to pry open his stepfather's eyelids in order to examine the pupils. They were completely normal: neither fixed nor dilated like they had been on the Knightleys' first case, when Clive had been under the influence of the Combination's murderous handbook, *The Code*. Clive was as obnoxious as ever, but he posed no apparent threat.

Jackie turned remorsefully to Darkus, who nodded. "He seems fine, but I think it's best for both of you if you check into your room and stay there until I contact you. Don't answer the door. To anyone."

Clive huffed, but something in Darkus's eyes told Jackie he was serious.

"Okay, Doc. We'll do that."

"Thanks, Mom. If you need us, we'll be in the presidential suite."

"The *what*?!" Clive roared.

Darkus watched from a discreet vantage point behind a sphinx as his mother and stepfather checked in at reception. Clive gesticulated wildly, clearly trying to upgrade their room to as close to presidential as possible, before giving up, his arms dropping to his sides like a Neanderthal as he trudged after Jackie and the bags. They entered the elevator, pressed a button, and ascended to what Darkus calculated was the twenty-first floor. They exited the glass pod and walked to a room halfway along the corridor.

Darkus made a mental note and continued staking out the hotel lobby, where, after a long ten minutes, Mr. Presto marched out of the casino in the company of several fawning hotel employees. Darkus shrank behind the mock-ancient stone facade and watched as Presto opened his arms to greet a small delegation of men and women in business suits. The figures looked familiar to Darkus. Plundering his encyclopedic knowledge once more, his eyebrows inadvertently raised as he picked out a former British cabinet minister, a female media baron, a disgraced Swiss bank boss, and a prominent American crime figure, among several others that he couldn't immediately place. In other words, a dragon's den of VIPs.

Glad-handing each in turn, Presto guided the group into an elevator, stabbed a button, and they ascended the incline. Through the glass, Darkus watched Presto and the delegation admire the view; then the pod slowed, reaching the notorious thirteenth floor—the same one that Chloe, or "Pam Clorr," had exited on. The group stepped out. Darkus narrowed his eyes to see which direction they were going. But he saw no further evidence of them at all. Just like Chloe, they had completely vanished.

Something strange *indeed* was afoot on the thirteenth floor.

Darkus crossed to the opposite elevator, swiped his presidential key card, and ascended to the penthouse level, stepping out into a luxurious, carpeted corridor leading to a pair of grand double doors. He swiped his card again and entered the presidential suite.

Tilly was sitting at a walnut desk staring at her phone, which was plugged into a charger in the wall. She had evidently showered because her hair had changed color again: from blond to an auburn red. She caught Darkus staring at it.

"It's my natural color," she admitted.

Uncle Bill was roaming back and forth by the imposing floor-to-ceiling windows, which leaned inward toward the apex of the pyramid. Outside, the Vegas skyline strobed and twinkled with a multiverse of lights, but in the distance a storm system was amassing, sending ominous clouds scudding over the hills. Summer storms were uncommon, but the desert was a law unto itself. Darkus caught sight of a jagged vein of chain lightning. Half a minute later a rumble of thunder arrived over the hotel. The same thing happened again, and Darkus counted a twenty-five-second interval between the lightning and the thunder, indicating that the storm was approximately five miles away and heading in their direction.

Dougal was playing nurse in the master bedroom, where Knightley Senior was stretched out, still unconscious. The Scotsman distracted himself by watching a huge flat-screen TV showing the countdown to a boxing match broadcast live from a nearby hotel.

Darkus called a meeting and explained quickly and concisely what he'd witnessed in the lobby and on the casino floor.

"Dad? *Here?*" Tilly protested. "That is *so* embarrassing."

"And Chloy?" Bill butchered her name. "That mad besom," he added, though neither of his junior colleagues knew what he meant.

"And Presto," said Darkus. "And possibly others."

"What's going on, Doc?" Tilly asked, genuinely puzzled.

"I don't know. But the answer lies on the thirteenth floor."

"Then we best have a swatch," said Bill, rolling up the sleeves of his leisure suit. "Dougal, ye keep an eye on Alan."

"Aye, Monty," his brother answered, using his birth name.

"We must approach with extreme caution," Darkus advised. "If Chloe has adopted the name Pam Clorr, it's a fair assumption that Bogna is being held either in room

200

1301 or close by. If we are discovered, we risk compromising the operation and putting Bogna's life at risk."

Bill swallowed hard, his Fiji-sized Adam's apple rising into the fleshy folds of his chin, then lowering again. "That poor sweet hen."

"Well, what are we waiting for?" demanded Tilly, unplugging her phone.

"What about your file?" Darkus pointed at the timer, which showed twenty-two minutes, the digits steadily evaporating.

"A watched pot never boils," she replied. "Bogna needs us. If she's in this building, let's find her."

Meanwhile, on the twenty-first floor, Jackie was systematically unpacking her bags, her face betraying a sickly cocktail of unease, torment, and sorrow. On the other side of the suite, Clive had switched on the in-room stereo and was strutting up and down in his hotel bathrobe, snapping his fingers and doing little wiggles that Jackie suspected were dance moves. Clive swung his arms around, then appeared to point at his reflection in the windowpane and waggle a finger at it. She watched him, awash with pity.

"Do you think there'll be somewhere nice to have dinner with Darkus and Tilly?" she ventured. "Maybe somewhere with triangular sandwiches? We are in a pyramid, after all."

"*Seriously?*" Clive implored. "You want to bring along those two freaks on our big night out? Sorry . . . no deal."

Jackie stopped unpacking and stood still for a moment. "Clive, I think we should have a chat."

"Sure, babes. When we get home," Clive answered, ducking the question.

"No, I think sooner than that."

"Do we have to spoil the vacation with one of your 'big chats'?" He incorporated finger quotes into his dance moves, before glancing over his shoulder and catching sight of the frown etched on her face. His mouth dropped vacantly as he tried to find a compromise. "Tomorrow morning at the complimentary buffet breakfast?" he countered.

Jackie sighed and sat on the edge of the bed, staring into the flashing neon beyond the window and the storm clouds gathering in the distance.

"Hold that thought, I've gotta use the john." Clive stalked over to the bathroom. "That's American for loo, by the way," he explained cheerily.

"I know, Clive," she answered.

Clive entered the marbled bathroom and examined his nest of salt-and-pepper hair in the mirror. Despite the dye, the careful feathering, and the expertise of his *Winner's Circle* hair and makeup team (the "glam squad," as he called them), the hair situation was not improving.

Just then, he saw a small red light flashing on a phone

handset next to the toilet. He gingerly picked it up and sat down on the closed toilet seat. "Hell-o?"

"Clive Palmer?" an American voice asked.

"Speaking. Is this room service?"

"Do you know *The Code?*" asked the voice.

"Wait. What?" Clive stammered.

"Do you know the meaning of *fear* . . . ?"

The posthypnotic suggestion took hold of Clive through the phone, like a lasso around a bull, tightening a noose around his consciousness. "Yes. Yes, I do," Clive responded in a whisper, not wanting to alert Jackie.

"Good. We wouldn't want your recent change in fortune to reverse itself now, would we?" the voice warned.

"No. Definitely not." Clive shook his head quickly, feeling his brain flooding with thick, gloopy syrup: a sensation he hadn't experienced since his last encounter with the Combination's hypnotic bestseller, *The Code*—which had led to him being fired from his lucrative job as the presenter of *Wheel Spin*, and to attacking his stepson, Darkus, in what doctors described as a "psychotic episode." Now, Clive was struggling with the feeling of falling headlong into a deep, dark hole. He was being tugged like a helpless minnow into a whirlpool, his head lolling from side to side. "Tell me . . . what you . . . want me to do . . . ," he murmured into the phone.

A few minutes later, Clive emerged from the bathroom with a rictus smile.

Jackie didn't look up from the bed, her head hung low. Her bags appeared to have been packed and were sitting in a neat pile by the door. Clive ignored this small detail and blundered on with the instructions he'd just been given.

"I've got a very special night planned, Jax," he announced. "And the fun starts *now!*"

CHAPTER 20
THE THIRTEENTH FLOOR

Following the briefest of showers—and the sudden urge to re-outfit himself in tweed—Darkus left his father in Dougal's care and led Tilly and Uncle Bill into the elevator. He pressed the button for the thirteenth floor, but the number didn't illuminate. Tilly tried swiping her key card, but nothing happened.

"It doesn't make sense," she remarked. "The thirteenth floor isn't key-card protected. Only the penthouse level is."

Uncle Bill pressed the button until his chubby finger blushed a florid red. "It's no good."

"Can you access the elevator management system?" asked Darkus.

Tilly tapped at her phone and shook her head. "Weird. No signal on 4G or Wi-Fi. It must be shielded."

Darkus selected the twelfth floor, and the elevator obediently descended at an angle down the pyramid, the flashing numerals counting down. They reached the twelfth floor and the doors opened.

They stepped out into a long balcony corridor that connected the rooms, overlooking the grand atrium and lobby area below. Darkus quickly located a fire exit and pushed through the door into a narrow stairwell. He climbed the stairs two at a time to the thirteenth floor and pressed on the access door, only to find it locked. He took a set of lock picks from his tweed vest, which was the only tweed he'd brought along—apart from his ever-present walking hat (which he was also wearing, more for good fortune than for any practical purposes). He realized once again that he was becoming more and more like his dad: believing in superstition over logic. He tried to pick the lock, but it was dead-bolted on the other side. Perhaps the hat wasn't so lucky after all.

Darkus reappeared on the twelfth floor to report, "It's locked down. The whole floor is."

"What about rappelling down from the fourteenth?" asked Tilly.

"The pyramid's a sheer drop on all four sides. It's too risky," replied Darkus.

"Ah think I may have the answer, Doc," Bill volunteered, ushering them back into the elevator. He pressed the button for the fourteenth floor. The doors closed and the pod set off up the incline before jolting to a halt as Bill pressed the emergency stop button.

"Now what?" demanded Tilly impatiently.

"A bit o' keepie-uppie," said Bill, appearing to limber

up, performing a jumping jack on the spot, causing the elevator car to rock and shudder. Darkus and Tilly instinctively held on to the sides, and each other, as the cables and weights screeched and clanked in complaint from the elevator shaft.

"Are you sure that's wise?" inquired Darkus.

"Trust me, Doc." Bill reached up with both meaty arms and pushed open an access hatch in the ceiling of the elevator. "Ah achieved a bronze in the Scottish Highland Games," he announced, before adding, "in 1975."

"Which discipline?" asked Darkus.

"Caber toss," replied Uncle Bill. "Stay here and await mah instructions."

Bill jumped again, this time grabbing hold of the open hatch with his pudgy hands and heaving himself upward. His legs kicked out in circles, narrowly missing Darkus and Tilly, who ducked back against the elevator wall. Then the Scotsman spread his legs wide like a rock climber, pressing his cowboy boots against the opposing sides of the elevator to wedge himself in midair. It was a mountaineering technique called "stemming," but Darkus had never seen it done quite like this before. Bill heaved again, hauling his bulk through the hatch and ripping a long tear under the armpit of his leisure jacket.

"Aye, yer maw!" He wriggled again, and a rip opened up in the seam of his trousers. "Ah, 'n' noo mah bahookie."

Bill struggled, his legs flailing in all directions as he slowly

207

vanished through the hatch—not unlike a hapless swimmer being consumed by a great white shark.

"Now for the full bhoona." Bill floundered for a few more seconds before appearing to be vacuumed up through the hole.

"Bill?" Darkus called up. "Are you okay?"

"Aye, Doc."

Raising himself to an unsteady standing position, Bill stood in the angled elevator shaft, with steel cables extending above his head and a glimpse of the atrium visible far below.

"Mammy," he whispered, trying not to look down.

He wiped his brow and glanced up, seeing the heavy sliding doors to the thirteenth floor just above him. He then knelt down and inexplicably unzipped and tugged off both his cowboy boots, plunging his hands into them instead, as if he were planning to scuttle along on all fours. He flexed his feet in his sweat-stained socks, then raised his arms with the cowboy boots on the ends of them like the pincers of a crab. He aimed the pointed steel toe caps of the boots and inserted them into the narrow gap between the sliding doors. Then he proceeded to pry the panels apart, inch by inch, much the same as a fireman using the Jaws of Life to open a crashed car door.

Darkus and Tilly heard a series of grunts and clanks.

"Bill . . . ?" asked Darkus.

"Come on up, and don't hang about," he wheezed in response.

Tilly knelt down and interlocked her hands to provide a step for Darkus, who briskly climbed up and grabbed hold of the hatch, hoisting himself through it. A moment later, his arm reached down for Tilly, who grabbed it and elegantly raised herself up through the gap like a circus performer.

Darkus and Tilly arrived on top of the elevator car to find Bill's tartan-socked feet protruding from the sliding doors as he wedged them open with his girth.

"Climb over me," he ordered from flat on his back. "Coorie up, ah won't bite."

Darkus and Tilly did as instructed, climbing over Bill's quivering body and looking confused to discover him wearing his boots on his hands. After the teens cleared the doors, Bill pivoted his legs straight upward in a surprisingly supple yoga move, then rolled his knees backward over his head like a human cannonball, releasing the doors, which slammed shut; then Bill rolled up onto his stockinged feet again. His arms were outstretched, perfectly balanced, similar to a gymnast saluting the judges at the end of an intricate routine.

"Impressive," commented Tilly.

Darkus held up a finger to his mouth as a noise reverberated down the corridor. It was a door latch unlocking. The trio retreated into the shadows by the elevator. Tilly angled her smartphone camera around a pillar to see who it was. Darkus watched the phone screen, seeing a teenage boy emerge from one of the rooms wearing sunglasses, headphones, and a baseball cap. The boy closed the door behind him and walked casually down the corridor away from them. Darkus recognized the figure from somewhere, but couldn't immediately place him.

"I know that suspect," Darkus muttered.

"Mmm," Tilly agreed.

The windows of the pyramid rattled as the storm edged closer. Darkus's catastrophizer began ringing like a slot machine, then the penny dropped.

"He was a passenger on our flight from London," recalled Darkus. "He was sitting a few rows behind us, and was one of the first to leave the arrival area."

Uncle Bill cocked his head, confused.

"You mean he followed us?" asked Tilly.

On the phone screen, the suspect reached the other end of the corridor, turning a corner into the adjacent side of the thirteenth floor.

"I don't know," replied Darkus, "but I'm going to find out . . ." He crept out from behind the pillar, following the suspect at a distance.

"Doc, wait—" Tilly hissed, trying to stop his arm. "Remember, it's a *trap*—"

She fell silent as the power to the entire hotel cut out, plunging the corridor and the atrium below into darkness. A collective moan resounded through the building as games were halted and guests froze on the spot.

"What the—?" Tilly mumbled, then was quiet.

A moment later, the power was restored and the lights flicked on again. The casino continued about its business, and guests crossed the lobby and glided up the escalators.

But the corridor was empty. Darkus, Tilly, and Uncle Bill had all vanished.

CHAPTER 21
RAISING THE STAKES

Darkus wasn't sure exactly how he'd gotten there, but he found himself in a large hotel suite, dimly lit by overhead spotlights. Tilly and Uncle Bill were not in evidence. He looked for the door and found it behind him. He tried to turn the handle, but it was locked from the outside.

He controlled the rapid thrumming of the catastrophizer, steadied his breathing, and focused his mind on studying the features of the room. It was like a plush prison cell. The furniture had been moved back against the walls: a sofa, a chaise longue, chairs, side tables, and floor lamps—as if someone had been preparing for a party. But what sort of party, and why was Darkus the only guest?

He approached the huge, sloping floor-to-ceiling window and checked for any means of escape, but he was sealed in. The first raindrops from the imminent storm splattered across the outside of the glass, like someone blowing liquid out of a straw. He walked closer, examining his reflection, which was covered in beads of water rolling quickly, one by one, down the window. Then a silent flash of lightning illuminated something *behind* his reflection: the kid in the baseball cap was standing there, behind him, still wearing headphones and sunglasses.

Darkus whirled around, but before he could complete the turn, the kid tackled him, smashing him against the windowpane so hard that a fault line rippled through it, threatening to shatter the reinforced glass. The back of Darkus's head took the hit, forcing his chin down, compressing his neck, and sending a jolt through his cerebellum: the part of the brain that controls movement and balance. Darkus staggered, trying to find his feet and recover himself, but the room was spinning. He was too shocked to speak. The catastrophizer was clattering like a helicopter losing height. His brain sent out a mayday call to pool its resources into self-defense, considering tactics and attempting to predict his opponent's next move. But his prediction was wrong. The kid wasn't interested in a fair fight or a varied style of attack. The assailant simply grabbed Darkus again and hurled him toward the same section of window with brute force, intending to send him flying into the abyss to certain death. A thunderclap shook Darkus out of his stupor. He had the forethought to grip onto the kid's arms and go with the flow, using one of the theories of Wing Chun: translating the momentum of an attack into a counterattack. Darkus sidestepped and swung his assailant into the glass instead. The window splintered, but withstood the impact. The kid's headphones were knocked askew, then he tore them off and tossed them aside in anger.

Darkus composed himself and had a split second to iden-tify the kid's face around the sunglasses. But it was a blur, and nothing clicked. Suddenly, his assailant was upon him again, this time with a barrage of heavy punches. Darkus retreated, dodging left and right, deflecting the blows with the sharp blades of his forearms, swiftly moving his left hand forward and then his right, keeping the attacker away from his center line, following the guiding principle of Wing Chun: protect the temple, the nose, the mouth, the solar plexus, the vital organs. But Darkus was out of prac-tice, and one of the attacker's punches connected with his jaw, sending him reeling to the floor. Darkus ran his tongue over his teeth to check that they were still intact, then looked up to see the kid towering over him, holding a large floor lamp in both hands like an executioner. Darkus instinctively rolled right as the marble base of the lamp slammed into the carpet, leaving a dent where his head had been a second ago. He rolled the opposite way as the weapon came down again, this time glancing off his temple. Blood started running down the side of Darkus's face, pooling in his eye and obscuring his vision. Darkus grabbed a nearby chair and flipped it upside down, using its feet to trap the base of the lamp, then jabbed upward, connecting with the attacker's face, knocking his sunglasses off.

A huge sheet of lightning lit up the room, bouncing off

the mirrors. The attacker loomed above him, and Darkus shook his head, not believing what he was seeing.

The kid's face was a patchwork of florid scars that had never fully healed. It had been carefully pieced together, but the doctors must have had so little to work with that the result was botched and monstrous. The eyes were too far apart, the nose was a mess of skin grafts, and the mouth drooped on one side into a sneer. And yet the face was familiar to him, as if from a nightmare.

"Long time, *Dorkus*," it said.

Darkus felt a chill down his spine. It was the voice of someone he *knew*: a classmate. Someone who had fallen victim to Barabas King's attack dogs during the Knightleys' previous investigation. Someone who had been so badly mauled that he was supposed to be confined to a clinic somewhere, being treated for life-changing injuries. And yet he was here now, with murder on his mind.

"Doyle . . ."

Uncle Bill initially thought he was experiencing an earthquake, or a particularly strong tummy rumble. Only when he was forcibly shoved through a dark doorway did he realize he'd been frisked and manhandled against his will.

When the lights came up, he found himself in a large hotel room, facing off with two heavily built henchmen, both dressed in black shirts and trousers, both wearing grim, indifferent expressions on their hardened faces. Bill quietly reached behind his generous waist and tried the door handle. Predictably, it was locked.

"A'right, fellas, so it's just ye and me," he began.

The henchmen stood with their arms folded across their barrel-like chests, motionless.

Uncle Bill looked around the room and casually reached inside his leisure jacket for his trusty Colt revolver, only to find it missing from its holster.

"So ye've taken mah mahaska too . . ." The larger henchman nodded and indicated Bill's gun, which was now tucked into his waistband. "Looks like ah'm outta luck then, aye?" The henchman nodded.

Bill's concentration was interrupted by a thudding from the en-suite bathroom, accompanied by a faint groaning. Bill took a moment to process the particular frequency of the voice.

"*Bogna . . . ?*"

The groaning rose an octave in response, becoming more insistent.

The first henchman moved to obstruct the bathroom door, but didn't expect the speed of Uncle Bill's knee swinging up into his groin area. The henchman doubled over in pain, and Bill smothered him with a bear hug before jumping into the air, extending all four limbs, and flattening him to the floor. The second henchman lumbered over to

216

assist his unconscious comrade, only to see Uncle Bill rear up to his feet again in a wrestling stance.

The second henchman charged Bill but bounced off the Scotsman's midsection.

"Here, have a Glasgow kiss," Bill said, and head-butted the henchman on the nose.

The two goons fell together in a heap.

"Boggers?" Bill called out, then kicked the bathroom door clean off its hinges.

Sitting cross-legged in the shower stall was Bogna, still in her vacation attire, her hands tied behind her back and her mouth gagged. "Mum-ty!" she mouthed, trying to articulate his birth name: Monty.

"Stop bumpin' yer gums. Ah'm here, mah wee clootie dumpling."

Bill leaned over gently to unharness her, accidentally turning on the shower with the shoulder pad of his jacket. Cold water gushed down over their heads, spraying everywhere and causing them both to shriek loudly.

"Baltic—! If it ain't a Scottish shower!" Bill cried, soaked to the skin, before adding, "Sorry, hen, mah fault . . ." He wrestled with the gag, removing it from her mouth.

"You took your times, Monty," she remarked.

"Ah'm not as young as ah used to be," Bill replied.

They looked at each other, both drenched and restricted by their dripping garments. Then Bogna yanked Bill into an embrace, so hard in fact that the Scotsman fell over and shattered the shower stall with his outstretched foot. Ignoring the cold water and the broken safety glass, Bogna's lips pressed against Bill's, resembling two goldfish squabbling over a pellet of food. Then they came up for air.

"Belter," panted Bill. "A'right, let's find the others and get outta here."

"Others, Monty . . . ?" Bogna's voice trembled. "Tell me you didn't bring Darkus and Tilly here?" Bill went quiet. Bogna shook her head, her face drawn with anxiety. "This plot isn't about me. It's about *them*. If they're here, they are in grave dangers."

CHAPTER 22
ALL IS LOST

Tilly woke up to find herself in a neatly appointed room with twin beds and a table with a plate of cupcakes on it. Her last memory was the lights going off in the corridor, and a falling sensation. Someone must have knocked her out. Confused, she looked around, finding the door locked from the outside, and no other means of exit. She quickly patted down her pockets for her phone, then breathed a sigh of relief, finding it in her back pocket where she'd left it.

She pressed the home button and checked the screen. The timer had reached zero, and she had signal. Precious seconds had already been lost. She urgently tapped an icon, checking her e-mail inbox. There was a message from Mike, her associate from the dark cloud. She impatiently stabbed the screen with her finger to open it. It read:

*T**
Dunno how to tell u this. It all blew up. The rest of the data's gone.
*^M^*

Tilly felt a disgusting, nauseous feeling in her stomach. If all this waiting had been for nothing . . . ? If it was all just a trick . . . ? She saw red; then raised the phone in her right hand and prepared to hurl it through the window, until—

The phone *ping*ed politely, informing her she had a new e-mail. She lowered her hand, tapped on the screen, and saw it in her inbox. Strangely, it had no subject heading and no sender. She stabbed the screen again to open it.

It was empty.

"What?!"

She repeatedly stroked the screen, faster and faster, scrolling down the contents, until a single-line message appeared at the bottom:

Are you ready for the truth?

Tilly felt even sicker. It was such a simple phrase, with so many complex possibilities. She scrolled farther, but the screen kept bouncing back up, indicating that she'd reached the end of the message.

She looked at the sentence again, and the letters evaporated before her eyes in a preset self-destruct sequence, turning to pixels, then to a blank screen.

"What's going on—?!"

She gripped her phone, threatening to crush it, then jammed it into her back pocket and looked around, helpless, her fists clenched. Overcome with hunger—for answers as well as food—she spotted the cupcakes and picked one up. She examined it for a second, cautiously, then took a large bite, giving herself an icing mustache. It tasted incredible. She took another bite.

Then, at that moment, a door opened in the wall. A door she hadn't previously noticed. She dropped the cupcake and cranked her head to see who it was . . .

CHAPTER 23
KING TAKES QUEEN

Dougal ordered his second dessert on room service, figuring that he deserved it after the epic trek through the badlands, not to mention attending to the every need of an unconscious detective. He checked his watch, then leaned back on the bed beside Knightley and stared vacantly at the large TV screen on the opposite wall. The boxing match was under way, and two muscle-bound fighters were pummeling each other in the ring, watched by several thousand spectators and several million TV viewers. Dougal's head rocked back and forth, imitating the boxers, dodging and weaving.

A TV commentator delivered a rapid, blow-by-blow account: "And he comes in with a jab, connects, inflicts some damage . . . This is turning into a street fight."

A second commentator responded: "That's right. What we're seeing is a *combination* of skill and roughhousing that is going to be very hard to defend against."

Knightley Senior grunted from behind Dougal, giving the Scotsman a fright.

"Alan . . . ?"

"The Coh . . . ," Knightley muttered. "The Combi—"

The first TV commentator carried on: "There's no doubt, it's a lethal *combination* of blows."

Knightley's arms suddenly raised up in a parody of a zombie coming back to life.

Dougal leaped off the bed, nearly tripping over himself. "Aye, mah auntie! Alan . . . ?"

Knightley's legs sprang to life, pivoted, and swung to the carpet, ready for action. "Bill?"

"It's Dougal," the Scotsman corrected him. "We came to save ye, Alan."

"Where's Bill? Where are Darkus and Tilly?" Knightley looked around desperately, then gaped through the inclined window of the suite, which was blurred by a film of rain and neon light. "Where am I . . . ?"

"You're in Las Vegas, Alan. *Sin City*. Darkus and Tilly are investigating strange goings-on on the thirteenth floor. Jackie and Clive are here too."

Knightley's brows dipped with surprise, meeting anxiously at the bridge of his nose, then raising inquisitively. He staggered from the bed to the closet, his limbs like jelly, barely supporting him. He located his fanny pack, his trusty tweed hat and coat, and began teetering on one foot, trying to clothe himself.

"I have to find them," he mumbled. "*Now*."

Moments later, Knightley spilled out of the presidential

223

suite, bowlegged and using the walls for balance, occasionally clutching his back, which was in several varieties of spasm following the unceremonious ride through the desert on the back of Dougal's horse. Panting with pain and jiggling from exhaustion, he found his way to the elevator and pressed the call button. The doors opened, and he selected the thirteenth floor. Glancing up, he noticed a discreet security camera watching him from above. Not surprisingly to him—though it would have been extremely surprising to his son—the elevator descended to the thirteenth floor with no problems, and the doors opened obligingly. Then, like a chess piece crossing the checkered board, Knightley stepped out.

The corridor was empty except for the bizarre and deliberately disorienting carpet design leading in one direction, overlooking the atrium, then turning a corner into the adjacent side of the building. There was no sign of life on this floor. No sign of cleaning staff or waiters delivering refreshments; no movement in any of the quarters.

"Doc?!" he called out hopefully.

He received no reply over the hubbub of the guests in the lobby below and the distant bells and whistles of the slot machines.

Knightley walked past the beehive-like row of rooms. He tried a few door handles but found them locked, then passed a suite with the door hanging ajar. He gently pushed it open as another thunderclap resounded through the pyramid. He edged inside, one shoulder at a time. His catastrophizer was thumping in his chest—for Knightley Senior had one of the devices too, which is where his son inherited it from.

As Knightley cleared the entrance, a lightning flash outside the window illuminated a bizarre romantic scene. His ex-wife, Jackie, was sitting at a candlelit dinner table set for two. Her current husband, Clive, was sitting opposite—except he was inexplicably wearing a hotel bathrobe with only a pair of trunks underneath.

"Alan, glad you could make it," Clive said in an oddly strained tone.

"Alan . . . ?" Jackie pleaded, strangely frozen on the spot.

Knightley approached with caution, glancing down to see that his ex-wife's ankles were tied to the legs of the chair, and her hands were tied to its arms.

"There's something wrong with him," she blurted, until Clive leaned over and clamped a hand over her mouth.

"Don't listen to her, Alan—I'm ab-solutely fine. Perfectly normal. Fan-ruddy-tastic, as a matter of fact."

"Clive, have you been reading things that have confused you again?" Knightley inquired gently.

"Read? *Moi?*" He shook his head. "Everything's confusing these days, Alan."

"Maybe you just need a break. A nice, long break in a mental health facility somewhere."

"I recognize that I'll never be the man you are," Clive

sneered. "Even though you're crazier than a bucket of bat guano. I know Jackie will never love me the way she loves you. I'm not a complete idiot."

"Well, you're at least half right," said Knightley.

"The thing is, Alan," Clive hissed, "I've got orders. Orders from my superiors."

"Clorr Entertainment," Knightley deduced.

Clive nodded. "They've made life pre-tty stu-pendous for me lately, and I'm not about to let anyone get in the way of that. Not you, not Jax."

Knightley swallowed, feeling the aftermath of his episode as tremors coursed through his limbs. He held the wall to steady himself. "I assume you're going to stop me from rescuing her then." He nodded to Jackie, letting her know his intention.

"Don't do anything heroic, Alan," she replied. "Save yourself. And Darkus."

"Don't worry," said Clive, "you'll all be checking out . . . permanently." He lowered his brows and marched toward the detective with a demented look in his eye.

"Can't we talk about this?" implored Knightley, but Clive charged at him, taking him to the ground in a stranglehold, demolishing an ornamental coffee table on the way down.

Jackie struggled with her bindings, hopping up and down together with the chair.

Clive and Knightley wrestled on the carpet, rolling over each other again and again. Clive appeared to be possessed of near-superhuman strength. He flipped Knightley onto his back, both hands locked around his throat, constricting the blood flow and restricting the oxygen supply. To make matters worse, a long string of drool descended from Clive's gaping mouth and threatened to land on Knightley's nose. The detective panted and blew at the string, trying to divert its course. Then Clive sucked it back up with an inhale before expelling a fine spray of spittle with the exhale, tightening his hold.

"Damn it, Alan," he moaned, "why do you and your son have to make everything so difficult?"

Knightley thrust his hips in the air, trying to buck the insane TV host off him, but couldn't. Clive kept riding the rodeo as Knightley shuffled backward across the carpet, his arms flailing for any weapon he could find. Clive continued astride him as they reached a heavy wooden cabinet containing a coffee maker and a minibar. Knightley managed to grab hold of it and topple it, turning aside as the entire cabinet crashed down on Clive, knocking him out of the saddle and dumping an assortment of beverages over him.

"Ouch, Alan!" he complained, rubbing his head, then examining his knees. "You've given me a case of third-degree carpet burn to go with it."

Both men struggled to their feet. Knightley assumed a Wing Chun stance, with one hand extended forward and the other held near his chin in a guard position.

"Hi-yahh!" Clive shrieked and performed a flying kick at Knightley, who easily deflected him, sending him ricocheting into a chest of drawers, which promptly splintered and collapsed under his weight.

Behind them, Jackie began hopping across the room in her chair, trying to enter the fray.

Clive got to his feet and charged again. Knightley turned his body sideways and extended his arm in an arrow punch that connected with Clive's jaw, sending another spray of saliva flying out the side of his mouth. But it had no effect. Clive kept marching toward him like a robot in a bathrobe.

Increasingly concerned, Knightley turned to his ex-wife, who was currently bouncing toward him in a valiant attempt to help.

"Mind if I borrow you a moment?" he asked.

"Be my guest."

Knightley picked up the chair, with Jackie strapped into it, and swung it around him in two full revolutions, picking up momentum, before slamming it into Clive—which had the threefold effect of smashing the chair to bits; freeing Jackie, who yelped and flew off into a sofa; and knocking Clive backward into a wall in a hail of plaster dust. But he simply brushed himself down, grabbed Knightley, and bulldozed him out of the hotel room, breaking down the door.

"Across the line!" Clive recited his catchphrase triumphantly.

The TV host kept charging out the doorway, back-flipping both men over the corridor balcony.

Knightley involuntarily screamed as he fell backward over the edge into the gaping abyss, before reaching out and grabbing hold of the balcony rail with one hand. He looked down into the atrium to find Clive clutching onto his other arm, his eyes wild and pupils flexing, his bathrobe flapping open, and his legs dangling in midair, thirteen floors off the ground.

Guests in the lobby below shrieked, looking up at the spectacle.

"Don't let go of my arm, Clive," Knightley coached him, hyperventilating. "The odds of surviving a fall like this are . . ." He performed a mental calculation. "Well, they're not good. Hold on."

"What's the point?!" Clive lost his grip on Knightley's sleeve and dropped another yard, greeted by a second shriek of horror from the crowd assembled below—either due to the impending fall or the view up Clive's bathrobe, it was hard to tell which. "It's game over, Alan! As usual, you win."

"Hold on, Clive . . . ," the detective repeated.

Security staff ran across the atrium for the elevators.

Suddenly, Jackie appeared like a vision above them, grasping Knightley's arm with both hands.

"Till death do us part, remember?" she panted, bracing herself against the balcony.

"Thanks, love," her ex and current husband both answered in unison.

"Did you mean *him?*" asked Clive.

"Or *me?*" asked Knightley.

Clive slipped again, screaming and grabbing hold of the belt of Knightley's fanny pack, which had the one advantageous effect of giving Knightley his other arm back. Knightley gripped the balcony with both hands, slowly raising his chin above the rail, with Clive still swinging from his lower section like a pendulum. Knightley managed to drag himself up and flop over into the corridor.

Jackie grabbed Clive's hand and held him steady until Knightley hauled his attacker the last few feet to solid ground, where they both collapsed in a heap. Clive lay flat on his stomach, heaving from exhaustion, then scrambled to his feet to find Jackie standing before him.

"Thanks for that, sweetie," Clive tittered, adjusting his hair.

"Don't mention it." Jackie aimed a punch and knocked him out cold.

She knelt down to find Knightley wheezing, prostrate on his back. She quickly checked his pulse. "Alan . . . ?" She bent over him, concerned, preparing to give mouth-to-mouth resuscitation.

Then Knightley leaned up and planted a kiss on her lips. Caught off guard, she responded, then stopped herself.

"Alan!" she said, recoiling in shock.

"Yes?" he replied, without apology.

"What do you think you're doing?"

"I just had a near-death experience. I think I saw the light."

"Well, we're not man and wife anymore. We haven't been in years."

"If we make it out of here alive, would you be willing to reopen that case?" he asked.

She paused, confused. "Do you really think this is the time?"

"Is that a maybe?" he pressed her.

"Maybe."

"You mean, maybe it's a maybe?"

"You're the detective, you work it out."

A fire exit burst open and a team of concerned hotel security guards rushed into the corridor.

Knightley shook his head, coming to his senses. "You're right, this isn't the time. I have to find our son."

He let go of her and she sagged, a little weak in the knees. Knightley jumped to his feet and jogged off down the corridor, leaving his ex-wife presiding over Clive's unconscious body. Halfway down the corridor, the detective stopped and turned back. "One more thing," he called out. "I suggest you check out of this hotel—at once!"

"I don't understand," the head of security puffed as he reached Jackie. "The elevator's not stopping at this floor. We had to break the doors down."

"I don't understand either," she replied.

The head of security helped her to her feet, then a massive, dripping Scotsman made his way through the staff, arriving at Jackie's side.

"Hoots, Jax," Bill wheezed.

"Bill? What happened to *you?*" She looked him up and down.

"Ah've found Bogna."

"You have?"

"Aye, we were just in the shower."

"Well, where is she now?"

"Downstairs with Dougal. We've got to get outta here."

"What about Darkus and Tilly?"

"Ye'll have to leave it to Alan. They're all in the hands of fate now."

CHAPTER 24
THE HAND IS DEALT

Darkus faded in and out of consciousness. Brendan Doyle towered over him—his arms and legs spread apart, as coiled and ferocious as the canine beasts that had savaged him.

"I hold *you* responsible, *Dorkus*," he spat.

Darkus raised himself to his feet, wiping a rivulet of blood from his brow but unable to stem the flow. "We couldn't possibly have known that by using your phone we'd incriminate you . . . that Barabas King would set the dogs on you. Is that what this is about? A simple matter of revenge?"

"Revenge?" Doyle laughed. "It was the best thing that ever happened to me. It gave me a purpose. The Combination has given me a purpose."

"They recruited you?"

Doyle nodded.

"To do what?" Darkus asked.

"To destroy you."

"Don't you see . . . it's all a game," replied Darkus. "This is a test of some kind. They're manipulating all of us."

"I don't care—" Doyle kicked, planting his right sneaker in Darkus's chest and propelling him backward across the floor. Then Doyle ran and booted him again like a football, catching him in the ribs, sending him rolling across the carpet in agony.

Darkus's vision flashed white with pain as the intercostal muscles around his chest felt like they'd transformed into six-inch needles. Then he experienced something even more terrifying: Doyle picked him up like a child. Darkus felt his entire weight in the attacker's hands. Doyle staggered toward the damaged section of window, then kicked at it, over and over again, forming a decent-sized hole. A fine mist of rain sprayed through the gap onto Darkus's face, reminding him how high they were.

Then he heard a faint noise in the corridor.

"Doc . . . ?" It was his father's voice.

"Dad?!" Darkus shouted back, but it was too late.

Doyle kicked once more, shattering a body-sized opening in the windowpane. Like a babe in arms, Darkus gaped up at Doyle's neck, which was crosshatched with scars and pulsing with blood from his exertions. It wouldn't have been surprising to find a Frankenstein-like screw protruding from it. Then Darkus realized: the *neck*. It was on the vital center line. It was still vulnerable, even though the attacker was in total control. Darkus weakly formed the fingers of his right hand into a jab. Doyle started rocking back and forth, as if he was cradling him. Darkus felt one swing, then a second, knowing the third meant he was going through the window. Doyle entered the final swing, just as—

Darkus thrust his fingers upward into the soft hollow of Doyle's neck between the Adam's apple and the sternum: known as the "jugular notch." Darkus briefly felt his opponent's pulse through the skin, then Doyle choked, gasping for breath, and instantly dropped Darkus to the floor.

Darkus winced and painfully rolled to one side as Doyle sank to his knees, clutching his throat.

"You're not dying," the young detective explained. "Your windpipe is compressed, and you're losing consciousness."

Doyle fell to the carpet, realizing that Darkus was correct. This was Doyle's last thought before descending into total unconsciousness.

Darkus dragged himself to his feet, feeling a stabbing pain in his ribs with each breath. He left his former classmate on the floor and staggered to the door.

Outside, Knightley Senior heard a persistent hammering from one of the rooms. He went door-to-door until he located it, then shouted: "Stand back!"

Knightley kicked hard, breaking down the door and finding his son wounded on the other side.

Knightley hugged him hard, until Darkus yelped with pain and his father let go.

"I've either bruised my intercostal muscles or fractured a rib," Darkus noted. "Or both. It'll require an X-ray to confirm the diagnosis."

Knightley looked his son in the eyes and kissed him on the forehead. "But you're *alive!*" He spotted Darkus's opponent out cold on the carpet, then guided his son out of the suite.

Darkus looked up and down the corridor. "Where's Tilly?"

Knightley shook his head. "I don't know."

Just then, a welcoming *bing* sounded from a nearby elevator. They both turned to observe it as the doors slid open. But no one stepped out. The Knightleys both waited, hearing the pounding of their own hearts. The doors remained open, bidding them to enter.

The duo looked at each other, unsure what to do.

Then they jumped as a macho American voice came over a PA system in the corridor: "Alan, Darkus . . . You have entered the Winner's Circle. Step into the elevator to claim your prize."

"It's a trap," warned Darkus. "We always knew it was."

The message repeated eerily: "Alan, Darkus . . . You have entered the Winner's Circle. Step into the elevator to claim your prize."

"But is it better to run from your enemy . . . or to face them head on?" asked his father.

"For once, I believe you're correct," confessed Darkus. "We must face them head on."

"Me? Correct? Can I have that admitted into evidence?"

Darkus didn't answer, feeling the full weight of fate upon them. He stayed shoulder-to-shoulder with his father as they approached the waiting pod and stepped over the threshold. The doors quickly slid shut behind them, and the elevator ascended.

CHAPTER 25
WHERE THE CARDS FALL

Darkus watched the numbers flicker, with each ascending floor bringing a sinking sense of dread. They passed the penthouse level and continued traveling upward.

"How high does this go?" asked Darkus.

"All the way to the top, I guess," his father responded.

The elevator slowed, coming to a halt. The doors slid open to reveal a silent chamber, shrouded in darkness. The Knightleys stepped out, remaining close to each other, finding strength in numbers, even if that number was only two. Darkus tried to focus in the gloom, observing the four sides of the pyramid, meeting in an apex over what appeared to be a boardroom of some kind. The inclined windows were so high up that the only view was of thunderclouds.

Two henchmen dressed in black emerged from the shadows, holding fluorescent handheld security scanners. They swept them over the Knightleys' bodies, top to toe, until the devices displayed a green light, prompting the men to lower them and nod to the unseen occupants of the room.

A flash of lightning illuminated some thirty figures sitting around a long conference table in the center of the room.

"Hello, Alan . . . Darkus," a familiar sneer rang out, as one of the figures stood up.

"Good evening, Presto," replied Knightley, recognizing his outline.

Darkus watched the theatrically dressed villain lean on the conference table, his Spanish gaucho hat tipped at a jaunty angle, with a feather in the band. A set of sconce lights dimmed up around the room to reveal the rest of the conference members, including the former British cabinet minister, the female media baron, the prominent American crime figure, and several others whom Darkus recognized from Web pages and newspapers but couldn't immediately identify. Whoever they were on any other day, Darkus knew that he was now in the presence of the shadowy organization that had haunted his family, and the world, since before he was born.

"Glad you could make it to our little get-together," remarked Presto with a high giggle.

"So this is the Combination . . . ," said Darkus, more to his father than to the rogues' gallery assembled before them.

His father nodded gravely.

"As usual, your assumption is correct, Doc," Presto answered. "And guess what? You're the guests of honor." He suppressed another giggle. "This is our annual conference," he announced. "Minus our former number one, Underwood, of course, thanks to your little operation on Harley Street. He's of no use to us now."

"So this *was* a game all along," Darkus addressed the conference. "To get us here . . . now."

Presto nodded. Knightley Senior remained tactfully silent.

"It was Morton's idea," Presto explained, referring to his boss. "If you ever caught him—which you did—the game would commence. And you followed the trail like obedient little mice." Presto made scampering motions with his leather-gloved fingers. "Three blind mice," he added, pleased with his description. "Creeping straight into the mousetrap."

Darkus recalled the chain of events: "First Bogna goes missing," he noted. "Abducted by Sturgess, the paid actor. Then we arrive, and nearly perish in the rental car . . ."

"All a test. Arranged by us," Presto said proudly.

"Then we followed the clues through the desert to Survival Town, Area 51, Vegas . . . past Clive, and Doyle, to here," Darkus carried on. "But what if we didn't make it? We could have failed at every turn?"

"But you didn't," Presto replied. "Vegas is the city of games, and you played yours so exceptionally well."

"But *why* . . . ?" asked Darkus. "What's this all about?"

Presto gestured like a mime, holding a finger to his lips, suggesting he couldn't tell. Not yet.

Darkus desperately searched his mind and his surroundings for answers. He spotted his former adversary, Chloe Jaeger, who smiled and winked cheerfully from her seat.

"And I suppose you're 'Pam Clorr' of Clorr Entertainment," observed Darkus, trying to build his case.

Chloe, followed by Presto, both *shook their heads*.

"Wait a second . . ." Darkus felt his previous hypothesis explode, his train of thought derail. He had to reassemble the pieces of the case into a new explanation for the facts. He spotted an *empty seat* at the head of the conference table. With Underwood out of action, there had to be a new head of the Combination: a new number one. "Pam Clorr. *Pamela Clorr*," he murmured, turning the name over in his mind, watching the letters separate and fall apart, before rotating like a small constellation, reordering themselves around the orbit of a new idea.

His thought process suddenly stopped in its tracks, freezing his entire body on the spot. It was an *anagram*—something so obvious and simple, and yet so impossible to believe. The whole investigation had been a trap from the very beginning.

"Where's Tilly?" he demanded of the room. "Where is she?" he shouted more urgently.

No one answered.

Darkus turned to his dad, grabbing him by the arm. "Dad? Pamela Clorr is an anagram . . . of *Carol Palmer*."

"I realize that." Knightley nodded toward a doorway at

the back of the room, where two figures were standing: one taller, one smaller in stature.

"Tilly?" Darkus called out.

"I'm okay, Doc," her voice came back, quavering and broken. "I've found Mom. Look . . ."

The figures emerged, resolving into Tilly and an attractive woman in her late forties with locks of curly auburn hair, tied back neatly, in keeping with her tailored business suit. There was something familiar about her features: the striking eyes, the dimples on either side of her mouth. Without the need for deduction, Darkus knew instinctively that this was Carol: *Tilly's mom.*

Darkus spun to his father accusingly. "You *knew?*"

"I knew that Carol had joined the Combination in the months before her death. She was helping me locate Underwood after his disappearance. Then I found out she was collaborating with him. I could only deduce that she had fallen under the spell of *The Code* herself." Knightley stared across the room at his former assistant and once trusted friend, Carol Palmer—the sight of her and the memory of everything becoming almost too much to bear.

"I did what my conscience instructed me to do, Alan," she answered calmly.

"To fake your own death and abandon your only daughter? I can believe a lot of things, but that one's hard to swallow. It must have been covered up at the highest levels—doctors, coroners, law enforcement. And most of all, in your own *heart*, or what's left of it."

Darkus watched, lost for words. He looked to Tilly, desperately trying to read her expression, as if it were the ultimate case to crack, but it was too complex—and perhaps Tilly couldn't make sense of it either. Her eyes were wet, her mascara running, but the tears were as much fear as joy. Her face had the troubled innocence of a child who'd opened their long-awaited Christmas gift only to find it was something entirely different—something terrifying: a Pandora's box, the contents of which she could not unsee.

Carol ignored Knightley and addressed his son directly: "I imagine you have a burning question, Doc . . . You want to know why you're here, yes?"

Darkus looked to Tilly again, receiving no feedback.

"The answer is simple," Carol went on, her face implacable. "You've completed the game, and now it's time to receive your reward. We'd like to make you an offer . . . *Join us*."

Darkus looked at Tilly, expecting a signal, something to indicate that they were still on the same side. *Weren't they?*

"You must be joking," Knightley Senior blurted. "You might have us in a corner this time, but we're not stupid. Or immoral."

"No offense, Alan, but your black-and-white ideas of right and wrong are outdated. It's all shades of gray now. And whether you join us, or not, is irrelevant. I convinced Underwood to let you live, albeit in a coma state for all those years. It was Darkus who resurrected your career and became the single biggest threat to our organization. That's why, with all due respect, it is Darkus we want on our side." She appealed to the junior detective. "With or without your father."

"We come as a package," replied Darkus, indicating his dad and Tilly. "*Three of a kind.*"

"Tilly has already made her decision, haven't you, darling?" Carol put a hand on her daughter's shoulder. "She's already got so much of me in her. It's hard to believe she didn't connect the dots sooner."

Tilly felt her mother's touch but didn't move, like an injured animal too traumatized to react, even to apparent affection.

Undaunted, Carol pressed on. "Darkus, we're offering you a position in the Combination. It's a one-time offer, and it comes with complimentary membership to some of the most exclusive clubs and organizations in the world, along with access to cutting-edge technology and paranormal phenomena, the likes of which most people couldn't even imagine."

Presto and the assembled villains around the table nodded knowingly.

"But for what motive?" countered Darkus. "To line your pockets, protect the interests of a chosen few, and fuel your own greed for power?"

"Bravo, son," declared Knightley. "Honor may be an old, outdated word, but I'm old and outdated, and I like it."

"Think carefully, Doc," murmured Carol.

"And what if I refuse?" Darkus put it to them.

Carol looked disappointed. "You and your father won't leave this room alive," she replied evenly.

Tilly shifted awkwardly, feeling her mother's caress on her shoulder—and seeing a compact pistol in her mother's other hand, trained across the room on her colleagues and friends, the Knightleys.

"Don't worry, sweetie," Carol soothed her daughter. "They'll make the right decision."

Tilly stared at Darkus, her eyes unflinching.

Darkus turned to his father for guidance.

"Well, while the kids are making up their minds, I've got a proposal of my own," said Knightley and swiveled his fanny pack around to the front of his waist.

Darkus looked at him, confused. The Combination members shifted nervously in their seats as Carol retrained the pistol, targeting Knightley specifically.

"It's okay, they're clean," she reassured the assembly.

"It's just a little something," Knightley went on, "that's old and outdated, like me, but it's constructed out of human bone and lined with lead, so it wasn't detected by your scanners." He unzipped the fanny pack and took out a small, finely carved *box*, with an array of cryptic-looking designs covering each side of it. "It turns out Underwood was quite a collector."

Darkus recognized it as a *puzzle box*—instantly deducing

that this was the same vessel used for Underwood's hard drive, which Tilly and his father had discovered in the vault on Chancery Lane.

"In fact," Knightley continued, "this puzzle box possesses many secrets. Some believe it even offers a portal into other dimensions. Other realities . . . Well, that's something you probably know more about than I do."

"I've got an easier way to transport you to another dimension, Alan. Don't make me pull this trigger," Carol called out.

Knightley carried on, in his own world. "I simply used it to smuggle something into this room. Knowing all along that we were walking into a trap, I needed an ace up my sleeve. Something I picked up in the hangar at Area 51."

Suddenly, a gunshot rang out in the chamber, and the shoulder of Knightley's coat opened up in a red hole, expelling a puff of tweed cloth. Tilly flinched, seeing a whisper of smoke rise from her mother's pistol.

"Dad!" Darkus yelled, grabbing his father as the elder detective fell to his knees.

Knightley grimaced but ignored the wound and arranged the fingers of his left hand in a wide spread around the box, covering the faces of the serpents and winged men that were etched into the design, then used the fingers of his right hand to rotate the petals of the flower engraving.

"The next shot will be the last," Carol warned him.

Knightley set the box on the floor as the device unfolded

246

itself. The lid flipped back and the four sides lowered with the aid of tiny cogs and wheels, opening up to reveal a small cube of clay-like substance, covered in wires, with a detonator positioned on top.

It was a *bomb*.

Darkus instinctively recoiled. Members of the Combination got to their feet in consternation and alarm. Presto choked back a nervous laugh and cleared his throat. Carol's eyes widened.

"Is that it, Alan?" she asked, trying to remain calm.

"It's enough to kill everyone in this room," he replied, resting his finger on the detonator, arming the device. "Now let's finish the game."

"You expect me to believe you'd sacrifice all the innocents in this building?" Carol challenged him. "Even if it means you succeed in destroying the Combination?"

"Dougal is downstairs with instructions to trip the fire alarm and order a full evacuation if he doesn't hear from me in . . ." Knightley glanced at his wristwatch. "Well, right now, as a matter of fact."

On cue, a fire alarm started bleating steadily throughout the pyramid. Seconds later, the echo of large movements of people reverberated up through the building. The Combination members began hurling threats and accusations, directed at one another as much as anyone else.

Presto and Chloe ran to each other, then checked the emergency exits, only to find them locked. Their eyes turned to their new number one, Carol Palmer, who had clearly ensured that no one would be leaving the room without her permission.

"Okay," Carol conceded, raising her voice above the commotion. "What do you want, Alan?"

"Darkus and Tilly, in that elevator now."

"You really expect me to give you my daughter back?"

Tilly shook her head, her face a veil of torn loyalties.

"Come home, Tilly," Darkus called out. "Remember what I told you in the desert," he pleaded. *"We're* your family now. *All of us.*" He nodded.

Tilly shook her head again, tears streaming down her cheeks.

"Don't listen to him," her mother instructed.

The entire Combination watched, paralyzed.

"You know it's the truth," shouted Darkus.

Knightley nodded tenderly to her. "He's right. He's *always* right."

Tilly spontaneously wriggled out of her mother's grasp and ran past the boardroom table to join Darkus and his dad.

"Matilda?" her mother shouted with an edge that made Tilly's blood run cold. "Don't put me in an impossible position . . ."

Knightley knelt over the box on the floor in front of him. He turned to Darkus and Tilly: "In the elevator. Now."

Tilly ran to the elevator and pushed the call button. Nothing happened.

"It's locked," she yelled back to the Knightleys.

"You know what to do," Darkus instructed her. "Hack into the hotel system and override it."

Tilly instantly took out her smartphone and began feverishly tapping at the screen to log on to the hotel network. "Got signal," she reported. Seconds later she had accessed the pyramid's floor plan and the elevator control system.

"You too, Doc. Go," ordered his father.

Darkus touched his dad's shoulder, then took his hand away, finding his fingers wet with blood. "I'm not leaving you," he insisted.

"If I take my finger off this detonator, we all go. Don't you understand?" Knightley whispered. "This is the only way to give you your life back. The life you want and deserve. Until we crack the Combination, you'll always be looking over your shoulder."

"Well, I've changed my mind," stated Darkus, tears blurring his vision. "I *do* want to be a detective. It's all I'm good at. I want to solve cases . . . ," he explained, then caught his breath. "With *you*."

His father's eyes welled up. "You've got your own life to lead now, Doc. You don't *need* me anymore," he added with a valiant attempt at cheeriness.

"Of course I do," Darkus pleaded.

"I always knew this trip was a one-way ticket for me. We did have some good times though, didn't we?"

Darkus grabbed his dad, refusing to let go.

Knightley whispered close to his son's ear. "Remember, Doc . . . what I told you . . . right from the start. If you *believe* in something, however outlandish, it might just turn out to be the truth."

Darkus looked at him, desperately trying to understand. "As usual, I don't know what you're talking about, Dad—"

"You will. *I love you, Doc,*" he stammered. "Now go, before I accidentally lift my right index finger."

Darkus shook his head, until Tilly appeared behind him and physically pulled him away. Darkus struggled as she dragged him toward the elevator, which was now waiting with its doors open.

Before Darkus could register what was happening, he was inside the pod and the doors were closing, blocking out his father kneeling on the floor by the bomb.

"No!!!" Darkus shouted through the closed steel doors, hearing his own voice echo back to him.

As the elevator descended rapidly, Darkus felt his stomach rise up through his throat, threatening to escape from his mouth. The gears of the catastrophizer screeched and clanged against each other like the speeding cables in the elevator shaft—processing its worst-case scenario *of all.* Darkus and Tilly sped down the incline, past storey after storey, each reverberating with the stampede of occupants leaving the pyramid in the midst of the thunderstorm. Until Darkus felt his knees seem to rise up through his spine as the elevator came to a halt at the lobby level.

The doors opened onto a scene of pandemonium. Guests and gamblers were flooding across the marble atrium toward the main exit. Among them were hotel workers in Egyptian garb, some guiding scared children. Uniformed police and security guards directed evacuees through the hotel forecourt and out onto the busy, rain-soaked Las Vegas Strip, where the blue-and-red lights of half a dozen police cars were already lining up in the mist.

Darkus and Tilly made their way through the throng, both lost in their own ways, both simply following the herd. Darkus saw the traffic being blocked off and onlookers gazing up at the pyramid. The surrounding hotels continued to strobe with powerful light displays. Darkus made out a large shape standing by one of the patrol cars.

"Bill . . . ," he muttered, breathless, taking Tilly by the hand.

Uncle Bill peered up at the hotel with one arm around Bogna and the other around Jackie, in a tight huddle. Then he saw the two teens stumble out of the crowd. "Doc! Tilly!"

A huge fire engine blasted its horn and pulled into the forecourt.

Darkus hyperventilated, grabbing Bill and his mom, trying to shout over the noise. "It's Dad! He's up there, on the top fl—"

Before Darkus could finish, a massive explosion lit up the sky, reflecting off the panes of the surrounding

251

buildings. Cops drew their guns; onlookers screamed, then took cover as the blast blew out the sloping windows on the top floor of the pyramid, sending a hail of fragments in four different directions. As dust and glass rained down over the Strip, it revealed that the apex of the pyramid had been completely destroyed, leaving the rest of the building intact. A thin wisp of smoke curled up from the summit.

Darkus stared up into the sky, raindrops splatting into his eyes, which were blinking in shock and disbelief. He opened his mouth, but no sound came out. Tilly managed a heart-rending scream. Jackie quickly grabbed both of them, trying to turn their faces away, but they refused.

Darkus watched as the world started turning before his eyes. The walls of the adjacent buildings began to slant and distort; firemen in high-visibility jackets ran inside the smoking pyramid, which took on even greater proportions, stretching in all directions, threatening to completely consume him. The thunderclouds warped and shuddered. The lights of the hotels elongated into long, continuous streaks. His eyes rolled back, and he felt himself starting to pass out.

Bill wiped his own eyes on his sleeve, then spotted something a short distance away, among a mess of glass shards and plaster. He ambled into the road and picked it up.

It was a tweed walking hat, shredded and frayed.

"Alan . . . ," the Scotsman whispered.

Darkus saw Uncle Bill holding up the hat in dismay and the final threads of his consciousness worked themselves loose. The last thing he remembered was the ground racing up to catch him . . .

CHAPTER 26
FULL CIRCLE

Five Months Later . . .

Darkus was never one to believe in paranormal phenomena. Maybe it was his mother's sensible nature, or a reaction against his father's bizarre ideas, which had been such a feature of his short childhood. But now, believe in them he must, and believe in them he did.

Following their return from America, Darkus and Tilly spent the summer together at Wolseley Close, doing their best to be ordinary teenagers. Clive had been confined, once again, to a court-ordered stay at a mental health facility, in Somerset this time. Jackie diplomatically referred to it as a "much-needed break," though Darkus suspected his stepfather would be away quite a bit longer than the phrase implied. *The Winner's Circle* had abruptly been taken off the air due to rumors of Clive's unacceptable behavior on set, and it was swiftly replaced by a nature program.

In secret, both Darkus and Tilly obsessively studied the

loose ends of their last case: an extraordinary one, which had taken them across continents, facing their darkest demons and their greatest foes, culminating in an explosion that had allegedly claimed the lives of every soul on the top floor of the hotel. Every soul, that is, except one . . .

Incredibly and contrary to all the laws of science, Alan Knightley had been found physically intact, three floors down from the explosion. He had been covered in rubble, white with plaster dust, and had sustained several fractures and a severe head injury, but he was alive.

His mind, however, was another matter. It had apparently retreated back to its protective state of trancelike unconsciousness. Uncle Bill arranged for a bed and the best possible care, courtesy of University College Hospital in central London. As word traveled, Darkus and Jackie experienced an outpouring of goodwill. Miss Khan brought flowers once a week. Even Chief Inspector Draycott delivered a box of chocolates and a Get Well Soon card, although his handwriting was so poor it was impossible to decipher—despite being studied by an accomplished young detective. Darkus suspected that even Draycott found life a lot less exciting without his father around.

Once Knightley had been settled into his hospital room and his every need attended to, Bill invited Bogna to take a spin on the London Eye with him. Having secured his own private capsule, at the top of the first revolution Bill plucked up the courage to dig into the depths of his voluminous overcoat and take out an engagement ring, which he then nervously fumbled and dropped—the fateful ring working its way ingeniously through a floor vent and plummeting one hundred and thirty yards into the River Thames below. After a stream of curses, followed by profuse apologies, Bill dug deeper into his overcoat and produced a large gummy ring from a forgotten packet of Life Savers, which Bogna accepted instead. They then embraced with such force that the capsule visibly rocked on its hinges, causing great alarm to the fellow travelers on the big wheel.

Meanwhile, Tilly found that her father's welcome absence gave her a chance to get to know Jackie better. Still reeling from the revelations about her own mother, Tilly routinely shared heart-to-hearts with her stepmom, often combined with visits to the hair salon. Strangely, Tilly started to dress more like Jackie, and Jackie started to change her hair color frequently and for no apparent reason. Tilly realized that perhaps the mother she had craved had been under her nose the whole time.

Under the guise of completing her homework, Tilly still followed the aftermath of the explosion via her online contacts in the dark cloud. Darkus suspected that—having discovered her mother had been alive all those years, albeit working for the enemy—it would be even more difficult for Tilly to accept her death a second time. It would take several more months, or even years, to retrieve and piece together the DNA from the scene. The familiar faces they'd seen around the Combination conference table had all been notably absent from public life: no photos, no reports. The same went for their former classmate Brendan Doyle, last seen unconscious on the thirteenth floor. It was as if the villains had vanished without a trace. Darkus convinced himself that the Combination had all perished—with the exception of Morton Underwood, who had slept through the entire drama, confined to his own hospital bed just outside London in a self-induced trance, and still under twenty-four-hour guard. But deep down Darkus knew that, lacking definitive evidence, it was just as possible that the Combination had *all* survived.

However, if there was a winner of the game, it was Darkus—for it had proved to him, beyond a shadow of a doubt, who he was: a *detective*, just like his father.

Through summer, autumn, and then winter, Alexis Bateman, still bedecked in tweed, took to arriving at the house with food packages for Darkus, claiming that his spirits needed lifting. Which spirits, precisely, was another matter—for the packages were often discreetly accompanied by books on the paranormal, with outlandish theories about everything imaginable, which Darkus consumed with great appetite, leading him to the inevitable question: how had his father survived the explosion? Had he hatched an escape plan that he hadn't shared with his son? Had he been provided access to another dimension? Or had he just been unbelievably, *extraordinarily* lucky?

Finding himself back in the solace of his father's hospital room, Darkus wondered whether he had stepped through another dimension himself. Or even stepped back in time to the events preceding his first investigation. For here he was every weekend, back at his dad's bedside, watching the gentle pulse of the EKG machine sketching a green mountain range across the monitor. Only this time, Darkus was joined by two other visitors . . .

Jackie gently squeezed Knightley's hand, carefully avoiding the tube running up the sleeve of his gown to an intravenous drip. Her former husband slept a dreamless sleep, except for an occasional flutter of the eyelids or an even more occasional flare of the nostrils. His hair was neatly parted, his chin was clean-shaven, and he looked younger than ever: the way he looked when they first met.

On the other side of the bed, Tilly kept vigil beside Darkus, both watching for any response from Knightley— the way a pair of fishermen might watch the still surface of a lake, waiting for a ripple that means the bait has been taken. They received no such ripple.

In the distance, Big Ben began its solemn toll across the capital, running in counterpoint to the jangle of Christmas bells that were presently ringing in the holy holiday. The bed was surrounded by gifts, which may or may not ever be unwrapped.

"That concludes our report for today," said Darkus. "The Case of the Cracked Combination is, for now . . . still open."

"When the DNA samples come back, we'll make sure you're the first to know," added Tilly.

"Well, the second or third, technically," Darkus corrected her.

"My bad," Tilly admitted.

"Don't beat yourself up, remember?" Jackie told her.

"Okay . . . Mom," she replied, still wincing slightly at the word, until it was met by a warm smile from Jackie that seemed to say: *one day at a time.*

Footsteps squeaked across the linoleum as a female nurse appeared through the door behind them, clutching a clipboard. "Time's up, I'm afraid."

Jackie looked up, disappointed.

"Merry Christmas, Dad." Darkus smoothed his father's furrowed brow.

Tilly squeezed Knightley's arm, then Jackie tenderly kissed him on the cheek.

"Can we leave the radio on?" she asked. "He loves Christmas music."

"I don't see why not," replied the nurse.

Jackie reached over and switched on a small radio by the bedside. A rousing performance of "Silent Night" rattled out of a single speaker.

Knightley twitched, and a brief flicker of consciousness

crossed his face, causing all three of his visitors to stop in their tracks.

Darkus felt a rush of expectation soar through him: the prospect of a new case; a new adventure; the return of his beloved parent and partner in crime-solving. But after several moments, with no visible change in his father's condition, the catastrophizer went quiet, and Darkus reluctantly put it down to a false alarm. He put on his tweed hat, then gently closed the door as the music came to an end.

The voice of the announcer came over the radio: "That was 'Silent Night' by Franz Gruber. The perfect combination of Christmas carol and lullaby . . . The perfect *com-bin-ation . . .*"